OUTLAW TOWN

OUTLAW TOWN

Lauran Paine

CHIVERS
THORNDIKE

This Large Print edition is published by BBC Audiobooks Ltd, Bath, England and by Thorndike Press®, Waterville, Maine, USA.

Published in 2004 in the U.K. by arrangement with Golden West Literary Agency.

Published in 2004 in the U.S. by arrangement with Golden West Literary Agency.

U.K. Hardcover ISBN 0–7540–6973–7 (Chivers Large Print)
U.K. Softcover   ISBN 0–7540–6974–5 (Camden Large Print)
U.S. Softcover   ISBN 0–7862–6543–4 (Nightingale)

The text of this Large Print edition is unabridged.
Other aspects of the book may vary from the original edition.

Set in 16 pt. New Times Roman.

Printed in Great Britain on acid-free paper.

British Library Cataloguing in Publication Data available

Library of Congress Cataloging-in-Publication Data

Paine, Lauran.
    Outlaw town / by Lauran Paine.
      p.   cm.
    ISBN 0–7862–6543–4 (lg. print : sc : alk. paper)
    1. City and town life—Fiction. 2. New Mexico—Fiction.
    3. Sheriffs—Fiction. 4. Outlaws—Fiction. I. Title.
    PS3566.A34O96 2004
    813'.54—dc22
                                        2004043796

Western
Paine, Lauran.
Outlaw town [large print]

CHAPTER ONE

THE TERRITORY

To get there it was not simply a matter of first receiving careful instructions from someone who had been there, although that was also necessary; it was essential to pass through the mountains without becoming lost, to survive the very intent and careful scrutiny of several vigilantes whose sole duty was to screen the riders seeking Outlaw Town, and also to end up where a man thought he was going, and not on down-country another twenty miles at Bellsville.

If it were decided on the spot that an approaching rider was undesirable the little green stones which guided people through the forests, over the rims, up out of the canyons and down through the softwood-meadows were simply reset, and the rider went right on by and kept riding until he finally arrived at the cow-town of Bellsville which was out upon the rangeland, twenty miles from the mountains and from Outlaw Town.

It did no good to complain down at Bellsville, because that revealed to the townsmen and stockmen of the range country that someone had been searching for Outlaw Town, which was the same as admitting they

1

were wanted by the law, and down at Bellsville there were nothing but honest and unsympathetic people. In fact, once a fugitive discovered that he had been rerouted, his wisest course when he came out of the mountains was not to go to Bellsville at all, but to turn in some other direction and keep on riding.

Sheriff Abner Wright of Bellsville had long ago developed an uncannily accurate sixth-sense about strangers arriving in his town from the direction of the high mountains northward.

For years people had been claiming that Sheriff Wright made more on rewards from fugitives he picked up riding on through from the mountain-country than he made in wages. Whether it was true or not no one knew excepting Abner Wright and he never commented, but as a matter of fact he had one of the largest and most complete collections of wanted flyers of any law authority throughout New Mexico Territory.

The people of Bellsville and its surrounding cattle country knew of Outlaw Town. Some said the whole thing was mythical and scorned the rumours. Others claimed to have known people who had wintered up there, or who had spent a summer in complete safety, so deep in the mountains at Outlaw Town there was no way for a posse to find them.

The talk had persisted for about ten years, and as a matter of plain fact Abner Wright had during the course of a number of apprehensions, got the whole story from disgusted fugitives who had been rerouted. Of course these men could not confirm from first-hand evidence that there was such a place as Outlaw Town because they obviously had not been allowed to see it, but Abner Wright had twice hunted outlaws down, had run them to earth and taken them alive, who had lived back there and both times the men told almost identical stories although neither could have known the other; Abner had caught them not just in different sections of his territory, but he had caught them four years apart.

Sheriff Wright was convinced there was such a place as Outlaw Town. Once, when a U.S. Deputy Marshal asked why he had not gone up there, Sheriff Wright had looked the federal officer squarely in the eye and had said, 'I know for a fact, Mister, that they have posters up there of law officers just like I have posters of outlaws, and they have my picture in their saloon. They probably also have your picture in the saloon. Now, if you want to go up there, I'll loan you a horse. But I'm not going—either with you or alone, or with a damned big posse!'

The men of Outlaw Town did not as a rule molest the people of Bellsville nor the ranches of the country surrounding Bellsville. The impression Abner Wright and others got was that there perhaps was an unwritten law concerning some kind of large perimeter around Outlaw Town, possibly for a hundred or so miles in all directions, which was to be inviolate; no one from the fugitive village—or settlement or encampment, whatever Outlaw Town actually was—was to commit a depredation in that area. It had to be something like that, because over the years a number of interested lawmen had compared statistics and for a fact, considering that there was probably more reason to expect lawlessness, in fact there was far less of it than there was anywhere else in the Territory.

To most of the cowmen, merchants, and the local residents in general this was a reassuring statistic. They nonetheless never—or at least very rarely—said they did not wish Outlaw Town, if it had to exist at all, did not exist in their countryside.

Clearly, the men up in that secret place were the most deadly and infamous to be found, and congregating a band of them in one place, unwritten law or not, was inviting serious trouble sooner or later.

Abner Wright did not concede this. His stand was that like a lot of other people he wished there was no such place, or if there had to be an Outlaw Town it was somewhere else, but he could cite the statistics to prove that actually people and their possessions were safer in his territory than anywhere else. Nevertheless, Abner was a good lawman : He did not like the idea of Outlaw Town and he liked even less the idea of notorious fugitives having a place—any place, anywhere—to hide in where they would be immune from apprehension, prosecution and punishment. Abner believed a man got in this life what he deserved. Abner also felt strongly that in some cases he was the tool by which miscreants were meted out their deserts, but if this seemed to imply that Abner Wright was an uncompromising, over-riding kind of gun-handy lawman, it offered an incorrect summary of Abner.

He had been a range-rider for the first sixteen years of his working life. He had become a lawman by accident, the way a lot of lawmen got involved in their profession; he had hired on to help keep a cow-town in southern Montana orderly one riding season, had developed a liking for the work—and the pay, which was better than the pay for cowboying, and the hours were also better—and he had drifted southward to become a constable in Wyoming, a deputy in Colorado, and now, in New Mexico Territory, he had been appointed to finish out the unexpired term of the sheriff of Durham County when the elected sheriff had died very suddenly in bed one night, while Abner had been his deputy.

He was tough and resourceful. He was not an exceptionally large nor beefy man, the way many lawmen were, but he was very knowledgeable about a number of aspects of his profession, such as fist-brawling, gunfighting, manhunting, and knowing when to look the other way.

He was not yet forty the summer that Deputy U.S. Marshal chided him for not going in search of Outlaw Town, and he still was not yet forty.

The man who ran the saddle and harness works in Bellsville, Clement Bowie, said he thought Ab Wright had to be about thirty-six or perhaps thirty-seven, but not a day over that latter age, and around town others agreed. They also agreed that he was a better lawman than their late deceased sheriff had been, and that he was also a very likeable man—which was a considerable compliment since most law officers viewed personal popularity as the least desirable attribute; they thought it was much better to have lots of respect based upon genuine old-fashioned fear.

Abner Wright's reputation had been built over the years upon his actual ability, and no part of it had been the result of a conscious effort to make a favourable public impression. He had no idea what a public 'image' was and his concern about public opinion was negligible.

He was an inherently responsible individual. He did what he recognised as his duty. The obligations which were required of him he accomplished and he was of the opinion that other people had the same obligations to be honest and orderly and truthful.

But Ab Wright, the man who had turned loose an eighteen-year-old professional horsethief in his second year at Bellsville, once told his superior, the late Sheriff of Durham County, that it seemed to him as though the world were full of people who had broken laws and who had neither been caught, or who had been stupid enough to keep on breaking them, and if during the course of a lawman's days he came across someone his innermost spirit told him deserved a chance, he not only had the right to offer that chance, he had an obligation to do it.

The sheriff had said very little, but he had subsequently confided in several friends that before summer was out he would have to fire Wright and find a more conservative-minded replacement for him.

Then the sheriff had died and the County Supervisors had appointed Ab Wright in his place.

No one appeared to regret the appointment a year and even two years later. There wasn't much serious crime, but when there was, Ab Wright was on top of it immediately, and his catch-ratio ran considerably higher than the former sheriff's ratio had run.

But compact, grey-eyed, sandy-haired Abner Wright had something else in his

7

favour; it was an unconsciously appealing personality. He was likeable, had humour, was generous with his time and his perspiration, and rarely seemed to be actually angry. He could dress down drunk range-riders, disarm them and if they needed it, whip them before jugging them at the Bellsville jailhouse, but even when he was in the thick of it, those who knew him best said he had not been angry.

It was difficult to imagine a man in Ab Wright's line of work being that even-tempered. It was possible his friends around town and upon the ranges over-estimated Ab, or perhaps even deliberately made him out to be someone whose unrealistic character was nearly flawless. On the other hand he had a few enemies, too, and even they would agree that they had never seen Sheriff Wright downright mad.

The man who managed the Durham County Trust & Savings Bank, John Lewis and who had been fretfully anxious over the possibility of his institution being raided by renegades from Outlaw Town for a number of years, viewed Ab Wright's good-natured disposition as one of the contributing factors to the eventual robbing of the bank that John Lewis knew in his heart and bones was eventually going to occur.

'Anyone who will allow desperadoes to congregate, even though they are miles deep in the mountains, is just too good-natured for a lawman's job. Ab Wright has simply been lucky. Well; my bank has been lucky then, but eventually those murderers and robbers up there will succumb to the temptation. I know they will. It's a lead-pipe certainty.'

Perhaps John Lewis was correct. The bank had been established seventeen years earlier and it had never been robbed, while a great number of other banks throughout the territory had been raided, but what was more likely was that eventually the law of averages would take care of the bank's flawless record, exactly as it took care of the flawless records of all other banks. Someday, the bank in Bellsville would be robbed. It did not have to have anything to do with Outlaw Town, it simply had to do with the fact that there was money in the safe at the bank and there were always shadowy men passing through whose interests lay in stealing wages not in earning them.

In fact, because Lewis's institution had not been robbed since its founding regardless of the fact that Outlaw Town was thought to most certainly contain many deadly and lawless men, was one of the reasons why Abner Wright felt that those men up there had some unwritten laws. He was also of the opinion that somehow or other they also had a way to enforce those laws.

Then the Durham County Trust & Savings Bank was robbed!

CHAPTER TWO

MANOEUVRED!

John Lewis was sitting at his desk slumped and perspiring. It had been a harrowing experience. Even if the pair of outlaws had not cocked their guns in the banker's face, had not menacingly promised to kill him in cold blood unless he opened the safe, and even if they had not stolen the bank's current cash-flow, which amounted to slightly more than four thousand dollars in silver, gold, and green-back paper notes, just the presence of those two men in his bank would have been a frightening experience, because John Lewis had never been a violent man and had never in all his fifty years experienced a violent interlude—until today.

'They were going to kill me,' he told Abner Wright. 'They stood behind me at the safe discussing how they would do it. One of them said a bullet in the back of the head while I was kneeling there, and the other said—no, a bullet through the heart because it wasn't decent to shoot folks in the back. Not even in the back of the head. Abner, I almost fainted. I would have fainted if I hadn't been certain they would have murdered me then and there in cold blood if I failed to open the safe.' John

Lewis regained some strength, and fixed Sheriff Wright with a hard look. 'Where were you? I've said it over and over again, sooner or later they would do this; they would come out of those blasted northerly mountains and do this. Abner, that money belongs to a lot of hard-working local folks . . . I'd like to hear your reason for allowing men like that to ride into town.'

Abner left John mopping his face and neck, went out where Miss Abigail the bookkeeper was perched atop the high stool at her desk, and leaned to say, 'Were they handsome and romantic, Abbie?'

She was a maiden lady of sixty and pierced Abner with a pair of very intent blue eyes, then made a slight sniffing sound. 'They were not; they were unshaven, dirty, scruffy-looking men.'

'Forty?'

'Twenty-five, not much older. Six feet or close to it. Nondescript except that the one with dark eyes had a small crescent scar over his right temple. And he was left-handed, Abner.'

Abner smiled. 'Anything else?'

Miss Abigail grew briefly pensive before saying, 'Abner; I know what Mister Lewis will say—that it's partly your fault for allowing men like that to ride free in Durham County.'

'He already said it, Abbie.'

'Abner . . . this is simply an old woman's

11

feeling; an intuitive sensation. Those men did not just happen in here today. Ordinarily we don't have more than four or five hundred dollars in cash on hand—enough to take care of pay-drafts and such like for the community. Today we had slightly more than four thousand dollars—and here they came, right on time guns and all.'

Abner's smile dwindled as he continued to lean and gaze at the bookkeeper. 'What's the rest of your hunch, Abbie—that someone who knew there would be four thousand on hand today, told them?'

She nodded, her bright eyes steadily boring into Abner. 'It had to be that, Abner, or a coincidence.'

'Why wasn't it a coincidence?' he asked.

'This is the first time since the beginning of the year—six months, Abner—that we had so much cash on hand. Doesn't that seem like an extremely unlikely coincidence?'

He didn't reply to the question. 'Abbie, if you saw them again could you identify them?'

'Could and would!'

His smile returned as he straightened off the desk. 'I love you. Did you know that?'

'Pshaw! Go about your business and leave me to go about mine!'

He went over to the safe. It was still open. There was a loaded Colt on a small shelf, which was not at all unusual. What *was* unusual was for anyone opening a safe under outlaw guns to try and use one of those hideout guns.

He sighed, thumbed back his hat and sank to one knee to look more deeply inside. Several neat stacks of papers were aligned side-by-side upon a high shelf, and there was a small tin box lying open. And the gun.

Abner stood up as a man spoke dryly behind him. 'Fine lousy to-do. I just put four hunnert savings for the company in there this morning.'

Abner knew the voice without turning. The man was Jake Farley, manager of the local stage depot and way-station. He was grizzled, humourless, slightly stooped and completely nondescript. 'Abner,' he said in that cornhusk-dry tone of voice, 'the company'll raise hell and prop it up.'

Abner said, 'Did you see anything, Jake; did you happen to notice anything at all?'

'Yeah; they come into town from the south. I don't miss many horses but I don't always pay much heed to folks. They come in riding a pair of nice stocky bays, tied up over here and come inside. I saw that much. Later, I saw them ride northward and they wasn't running like you'd expect robbers to do. I didn't have any idea, until old Lewis come outside squealing like a shoat caught in a gate. But I didn't see either of the robbers very good, Abner.'

'Came from the south and rode off to the north?'

'Neat as a pin,' stated Farley. 'Calm and orderly and neat. Come from the south and left by the north. Just as natural as you and I'd do.' Jake's rheumy eyes lingered on Sheriff Wright. 'Abner . . . ridin' northward, they was probably heading for Outlaw Town.'

Abner groaned. 'Don't say that to Lewis.'

Jake, like everyone else in town who'd had much to do with the banker over the years, understood about John Lewis's fixation concerning Outlaw Town. Jake shrugged. 'All right, I won't say nothing. But that won't stop him from figuring it out for himself. Even if he never finds out them lads rode northward, he's going to swear up and down . . . well, you know.'

'Yeah, I know.'

Abner went down as far as the general store and turned in. He was out of smoking tobacco. The grizzled, greying clerk who waited on him said, 'Glad it was the bank and not us. ' 'Course the boss wouldn't like me sayin' that, him having money in the bank and all, but I'm still glad it wasn't us.' He handed over the tobacco and papers. 'Did they really get four thousand dollars?'

'Really did,' replied Abner, tearing open the little cloth sack as he got ready to trough a wheatstraw paper and roll a smoke.

'I had no idea they had so much money up there,' stated the clerk. 'The bank must be rich.'

14

'Sure would be a nice surprise if a man was a bank-robber,' murmured the sheriff, lighting up and inhaling, exhaling, and turning to look out the front window into the sun-bright morning roadway.

The clerk agreed. 'Yeah; hell of a nice surprise. I'll bet they get disappointed plenty of times.'

Abner was not really listening. Across the road out front of Clement Bowie's harness works Lester Hardy, who had a saw-filing and gun-repair shop down near the blacksmith's place, was talking with one of the stage-drivers. All Abner knew about that particular whip was that he made the trip to Bellsville every other day, and that he never seemed to bring in his teams wet and blowing. Otherwise, the man was tall and rawboned-looking and perpetually bronzed from much exposure, and seemed to carry himself with that very erect, very proud stance of most professional coach drivers, who were a yeasty breed.

The clerk had to go across to another counter and wait upon a female customer. Abner strolled forth upon the plankwalk out front, watched Lester Hardy depart on his way to the bank, and watched that lanky coach-driver saunter towards the log gateway leading into the company's corralyard which lay south a couple of yards from Jake Farley's office.

Later, when Abner was at the jailhouse going through his carefully-maintained file of dodgers seeking a dark-eyed outlaw with a crescent scar over his temple and who was left-handed, John Lewis walked in. He looked much different than he had looked earlier, only a short while after the robbery. Now, he was nearly his normal self as he said, 'They rode northward, Abner. After they took all the savings of folks, they rode off in the direction of Outlaw Town. Did you know that?'

Abner put aside the dodgers he'd been studying and went to his desk-chair as he said, 'Yes, I heard they'd left town going north, John, but north can be a hell of a lot of different directions, can't it? No one said anything about Outlaw Town.'

'I did,' exclaimed the banker. 'I just now said something about it. Abner, I'm going to take it up with the Town Council tomorrow night at their meeting. Something has got to be done! Either we make up a posse from Bellsville and send it in there, or I'm going to contact the U.S. Marshal down at Albuquerque. If necessary, by gawd Abner, I'll contact the army. Now this has simply gone on long enough. We're all at the mercy of a congregation of the most infamous outlaws in the south-west. Today they took four thousand dollars. Tomorrow they'll murder folks. Take my word for it.'

Abner let the storm blow itself out while he leaned upon the box of fugitive-dodgers gazing pensively out a barred front window into the golden-lighted summer roadway. Finally he said, 'Mister Lewis, I'm interested in those bandits and I'm doing what's got to be done about them—but there isn't a darn bit of evidence to suggest they came from the mountains, or that they went up into the mountains after the robbery. In fact, they entered town from the south, not the north.'

'But what direction did they ride off in, Abner? I'll tell you. They rode north!'

'Yeah, and north covers a hell of a lot of—'

'Abner, I can't even guess why you don't want to go find those men at Outlaw Town, but it's going to be done even if I have to get the army to do it!'

After the irate banker had departed Abner continued to lean pensively gazing out the window for a moment or two, then he returned to the file-search, and because Abner persevered he came across a flyer without a photographic likeness but with a written description which fitted the man Miss Abbie had described. He had the little scar over his temple, was left-handed, dark-eyed and of medium size and build. His name was Curtis Custer Holt.

Abner pulled out that dodger, sat at the desk studying it, and when Carey Brookshire walked in smelling of heat and sweat and horses Abner passed the dodger across. 'That's one of them,' he said.

Brookshire sat, flung off sweat and read

aloud. 'Holt, left-handed . . . hell, he's a murderer. They want him in Arkansas and Texas and Missouri. Covers a sight of ground too.'

'John Lewis was in here waving his coup stick a little while ago,' stated Abner, 'complaining to high heaven.'

'Oh, that silly son of a bitch,' responded the blacksmith off-handedly while he continued to study the wanted poster.

'My point is,' stated Abner, 'that while Lewis was groaning and threatening, he had no idea how lucky he was. Look at the record Holt's got there : eleven robberies of banks, stages and stores, and seven murders committed. Mister Lewis had ought to be giving thanks.' Abner arose and stepped to the window, then turned back and said, 'I wish those damned fools had ridden south instead of north.'

Brookshire pitched the poster back atop the littered desk, and nodded. 'I understand; thing is, it won't be just that dumb-ass Lewis, it'll be half the town today and two-thirds of the whole blasted countryside by day after tomorrow. They'll all be sayin' those outlaws came from back in the mountains. Is that what you mean?'

'Yeah.'

'Any way to weasel out of it? Anyway, Abner, as a fact those fellers just maybe did come from up there. It's not impossible.'

Abner regarded his massive friend thoughtfully, then smiled and went back to the desk to start chucking dodgers back into their box. He very dryly said, 'Yeah, they could have.'

Brookshire had been on his way to the corralyard of the stage company to pick up a couple of horses and take them back south by way of the back-alley to his shoeing works, so his pause at the jailhouse had been only social. After he had departed, that shoeing-shed aroma he'd brought in lingered the rest of the day. Even tobacco-smoke could not dissipate it. It could momentarily overlay it but it could not kill it, and later when Jake Farley came in looking as solemn and dry and vinegary as usual, Jake wrinkled his nose but made no comment until after he had taken a chair, and removed his dilapidated old soil-and-sweat-stained hat, and even then although he commented he was being discreet.

'You'd ought to leave them front-wall windows open night as well as day,' he said, and moved ahead to the topic which had brought him. 'One of the company couriers who carry important light mail by saddlehorse, come in a spell back, and after folks told him what's happened at the bank he recollected seeing a pair of riders parallelin' the coachroad northward above five, six miles, heading for the mountains on an angle. Sort of westerly, Abner. He was sure it was them outlaws.'

Abner smiled. 'He was on the coachroad?'

'Yeah.'

'How far west were those riders?'

'Well, you know there's arroyos and what not directly beside the road for couple miles and—'

'That's what I'm getting at, Jake. He had to have been looking out there more than a mile and a half. So how could he tell it was that pair of outlaws?'

'Both riding bay horses,' said Farley, 'and who else would be heading into the mountains? Cattlemen hereabouts got no reason to; don't anyone run cattle up there, Abner. And those two would be expecting a posse to be on their butts . . . they wouldn't have any way of knowing the law down here was settin' on its haunches in the local jailhouse lookin' at pictures on old wanted flyers, would they? No. But they'd be heading for Outlaw Town. Abner, that's the best place for fellers like that to be heading.'

Jake continued to hold his fixed and impersonally rueful stare upon the lawman for a moment, then he rose, dropped the ancient hat back upon his head and walked out without another word. He was annoyed, but the only way to be sure was for someone like Abner, who knew him this well, to see the signs.

Abner rolled a smoke, swore at the empty

room, lugged his box of dodgers back to their corner and returned to the desk to sort swiftly and discard some papers while pushing other papers into drawers until the tabletop was clean. Then he went to the wall-rack, took down his boated Winchester, looked all around, cursed again at nothing in particular and walked out. He locked the jailhouse door from the plankwalk and turned southward.

He was mad. Not just angry but indignant and exasperated. Carey believed those men had come from the mountains, and Carey was his friend. Farley believed it, but Farley would have believed the worst in any case.

But Carey was right about one thing. Within a couple of days everyone through the countryside would be convinced those bank-robbers had come from Outlaw Town. Abner would bet good money they not only had not come from up there, but were not now heading for up there.

Of course, that wasn't the point. Put very simply, the point was that everyone believed those had been renegades from Outlaw Town, and that, of course, put Sheriff Ab Wright squarely into the position he had been avoiding ever since he'd hired on as a lawman in Durham County. He had to go up there.

That was a little like a man running inside a bear-den to see if it was inhabited. He knew for a fact they had a drawing of him up there because twice when he'd captured renegades from Outlaw Town they had told him bluntly how pictures of the nearest or most famous south-western lawmen lined a wall of the saloon up there.

CHAPTER THREE

THE DEAD MAN!

There were several ways Ab Wright could think of for reaching Outlaw Town. Perhaps a good way would be to cross the mountains then turn back southward and make the approach as though he were entering the mountains from the direction of Colorado. No doubt a good bit of the traffic to Outlaw Town came southward like that.

But what was the point? Even if he were in the mountains for a couple of days and hadn't shaved, he would no doubt still be recognisable to someone in there.

Another way would be to ride due northward on the stageroad, then cut inland, or westerly, across the lower reaches which were just below the highest rims.

Hell! regardless of how clever he attempted to be, they were not going to be fooled for very long, if they were indeed fooled at all, and that being the case the most reasonable route would be a direct approach.

It would be easier on his horse and it would also be easier on him.

He paralleled the coachroad and because there was nothing else to interest him he scouted for fresh sign, hoping to pick up the trail of those riders the stage-company's courier had seen. He did in fact eventually locate the fresh marks of a pair of horses being ridden side by side in the general direction of the foothills, and when he got up there he got a genuine surprise : he found a loose saddle-animal.

It was a tractable, well-made bay and it had the sweat marks of a recent saddling upon its back, and more fresh tell-tale marks where the cheek-pieces of a bridle had recently been in place.

The horse was easy to catch and allowed Abner to look it all over, even to list each foot and examine each steel shoe. Finally, as Abner rolled a smoke and squinted at the horse, the animal amiably gazed back, then turned and went grazing back among the little hogbacks and fat low rolling ridges of the foothills, with Abner watching its progress. Eventually, he left his own animal tied in some trees and went roundabout, back and forth looking at the trod earth where the stray horse had been comfortably grazing in and out among the low hills, until he came to a brushy crevice amid some bone-grey ancient boulders, and there he saw bootmarks. There too, after he'd discovered that most of the brush in the crevice was not rooted there and could be pulled out, he also found a saddle, a bridle, and a Navajo saddle-blanket covering the other two items.

He sat on a big grey boulder eyeing his discovery. Of course it was not unheard of for a rangeman to hide his outfit if he had reason to have to abandon it for a while, but to a man of Abner Wright's present turn of mind, this was no such temporarily abandoned outfit. Not when the horse had also been abandoned here.

Maybe that stage-company courier had indeed seen the pair of outlaws who had robbed the bank. That didn't explain the abandoned horse and horse-outfit, but there might somehow be a connection. Abner tried to imagine what it was, and when he eventually gave up and got down as close as he could to grunt and curse and pull until he had those three items of horsemanship on the ground at his feet, he had imagined a pretty far-fetched notion of two men riding up here after raiding the Bellsville bank, and one of them abandoning his outfit for a fresh outfit no one would be likely to recognise as ever having been in Bellsville, and heading on out.

But why hadn't they both changed identities, why just one of them?

He examined the bridle carefully, and the blanket, and finally the saddle. The saddlebags

24

were completely empty and they were the only real hope. As for the saddle it was like a thousand others; it had been manufactured at Miles City, Montana, was at least fifteen years old, and even if the maker were still alive and even if he remembered to whom he had originally sold the saddle it was a dead certainty at least five other rangemen had owned the saddle since it had been made and first sold.

Abner sat and smoked, and finally went in search of more tracks. What he found was the place where a pair of booted men had stood, apparently for some little time talking before one of them had got back astride and gone up into the mountains while the other one had struck out eastward in the direction of the stageroad.

This, finally, offered a pattern, and Abner pondered it as he went back for his horse. One of those outlaws had indeed gone up into the mountains, but the other one, Abner was willing to bet his wages, had gone over to the stageroad so that when he rode back to town his tracks would blend with all the other horse tracks over there, so he could not be tracked.

Abner felt like swearing. He pondered and sat his saddle looking southward towards town, and decided that without a doubt Miss Abbie had been right, by gawd; someone had indeed known there was a lot more money at the bank than there usually was. Someone down there in town had been one of those bank-raiders!

The complications arising from this development were instantly apparent. He could go back, or he could press on into the mountains. If he went back he'd better be able to locate the other robber otherwise the recriminations were going to start up again, and more pointedly this time, no doubt. Otherwise, going in search of Outlaw Town through the depths of a mountain-chain he was not very familiar with might take days, and meanwhile if the man at Bellsville had the money and decided to leave . . .

He turned southward riding back over the same general terrain over which he had earlier passed on his way to the foothills. He left the amiable bay and the horse equipment back there where he'd last looked at them.

Darkness arrived, eventually, and by the time he had his town in sight there were the customary lamps lighted throughout town. Ordinarily, he enjoyed riding back into Bellsville this time of early night; the place was so lighted up it reminded him of Christmas.

He went to the liverybarn and without offering any kind of explanation handed his horse over to the night-man, then asked if the nightman had had any other late-day arrivals at the barn. He hadn't. The nighthawk not only hadn't had any other customers this evening but he and the daymen had briefly conversed as they changed positions about

26

suppertime and the dayman had confided that it had been a very poor day; in the morning they'd only had a travelling pedlar stop with his rig and team, and in the afternoon only the clerk at the general store had returned from somewhere beyond town.

If conditions like these prevailed for the next ten or twenty days, the nightman confided, the liveryman would be fit to be tied.

Abner strolled out front, looked up the roadway where only desultory traffic showed, and most of that was near the saloon across from the harness works, then on a hunch he strolled into one of the east-side little back streets to a small cottage with a dilapidated white picket fence out front, and went up to lightly knock.

The woman who opened the door had one hand behind her back. Abner smiled down into her dark blue eyes. 'Miss Abbie . . .'

She straightened up slightly and stepped out upon the shadowy little porch. 'This is a fine time of night to be calling on folks,' she exclaimed, and put the big old horse-pistol upon a chair-seat. He said nothing about that.

'Miss Abbie, do you know the clerk who minds the general store?'

She looked slightly askance. 'Do you mean Douglas Whittier?'

'Yes.'

'I know him,' she said. 'What of it, Abner?'

'You said you could identify both those

27

bank-robbers.'

She stared. 'Him? You mean was it Douglas?'

He nodded and stood watching the lined face in front of him.

'Abner, it was hard to see both of them. What I should have told you was that the man with the little crescent scar over his right temple and who was holding his pistol in his left hand, was actually between his companion and me. I could see the other man, mind you, but it was a little more difficult and he had a handkerchief up to his face in his left hand.'

Abner felt like sighing aloud and scolding Miss Abbie, instead he smiled understandably. 'You're a big help anyway, and as soon as I get the left-handed one—'

'But you believe the other one was Douglas Whittier?'

'Maybe. Tell me something else, Miss Abbie. Had he been in the bank earlier or perhaps the previous day? What I'm getting at, could he have known there was so much money at the bank today?'

She answered quickly in her normal abrupt manner. 'Yes. Mister Whittier was in last evening, late yesterday afternoon, and all he wanted was some deposit slips from Mister Lewis . . . He could have known because Mister Lewis and one of the other employees were stuffing the money into the safe while he was there. I remember that very distinctly.'

'Take your hogleg and go back inside,' said Abner picking up the weighty big old durable horsepistol. 'Wherever did you get this thing, Miss Abbie?'

'My brother carried it through the war. He was killed during the Peninsular Campaigns and a friend of his passed through years back and gave it to me. It belonged to my brother, Jerome.'

He handed it back to her. 'I'm sorry, Miss Abbie.'

She started to make a curt comment, then paused looking up into his face, and after a while she said, 'Abner, I live with that kind of sorrow every day of my life. I pray to the good Lord you won't have to . . . And why don't you get married?' She made her little snorting-sniffing sound which seemed to be composed of equal parts exasperation and irritability. 'You're a fine-looking man. I'll admit the selection in Bellsville is not very good—but Bellsville isn't the only town in New Mexico, is it?'

He almost laughed, and for now he forgot how tired he was. 'You point me in the direction of one like you, thirty years younger, and you'll see how quick I'll get married, Miss Abbie.'

'Oh, go catch some bank-robbers. And for heaven's sake, Abner, be careful. Be very careful. I don't have the room inside me to grieve for another handsome young man.

29

Good night!'

She took the big pistol and went back inside, closed the door and he heard the bar drop into its metal hangers behind the door.

He did not know where Douglas Whittier lived, but he did recall being told by someone a year or so back that Whittier was an unmarried man, and that usually meant someone lived at the local boarding house, which in fact was also where Abner Wright lived, but around back with his own private entrance, and dozens of men had moved in and moved out without Abner knowing a thing about any of them.

He went up there and got old Tom Hurst away from his nightly pinochle session with some other old gaffers to ask if the general store clerk had a room. Tom pointed towards the gloomy stairway.

'Up yonder, second door on the north side of the hall. What'n'ell you want him for, Abner?'

'See if he knows how to play pinochle.'

'We already have a full table,' stated the boarding-house proprietor, frowning.

'Then go on back to your game,' said Abner, lightly tapping the older man on the shoulder as he swung past heading for the stairway.

There had never since Abner had known this great old barracks of a wooden structure, been adequate light upstairs. In fact there was rarely enough light downstairs but at least

30

down there some roomers left their doors
open on hot summertime nights and that
allowed more lampglow to reach the gloomy
corridor. But upstairs there was just one
hanging lantern and it was more than mid-way
along, so the room where Abner halted, then
leaned to listen, was in almost total darkness.

Someone was in the room. Abner could
detect small noises. He could not decide what
the man was doing to make those small noises
but he was satisfied Whittier was at home, so
he straightened back and lightly knocked.

For ten seconds there was not a sound. All
the activity beyond the door ceased. Abner
had his hand poised to knock again when the
door opened and the man who had sold him
some tobacco and cigarette papers much
earlier in the day was standing there without
his collar or shoes and with tousled hair and
slightly flushed face.

He recognised Sheriff Wright and said,
'Good evening, Mister Wright.' He looked a
little quizzical. 'Is there something I can do for
you?'

He made no move to step away from the
door and he made no move to invite Abner in.

The smell of cigar smoke was strong beyond
the door. The light was bright, too bright for
normal use and over the clerk's shoulder
Abner saw a rolled bedroll and a pair of full
saddlebags lying atop a bed which looked as
though it had been hastily pulled apart. He

smiled at Douglas Whittier. 'I wanted to know if maybe you recollect any strangers in the store today, or maybe yesterday. One of them would have had a little scar over his right temple, and I think he was left-handed. Maybe they'd come in to buy tinned stuff.'

The clerk slowly shook his head while eyeing Abner intently. 'Are you talking about the men who robbed the bank?'

'Yeah.'

'What about the other one? Weren't there two of them, Sheriff?'

'Yeah, but no one got a good look at the second one, Mister Whittier. At least all the folks I've spoken to up until now didn't have a description to give me; just that he was about the same size and build as the feller with the scar, and had a neckerchief or something like that up in front of his face. But I'm not through asking. I've still got six or eight more folks to talk to after I've finished here.'

'I wish to hell I could help,' said the store-clerk. 'I surely wish I could, Sheriff. If there's one thing needs stamping out it's robbers like that. They don't just raid banks, they also raid general stores and they kill a lot of folks . . . But I can't recollect a single stranger being in the store today or yesterday, or even for a few days before that. I wish to hell I could remember someone, though.'

He sounded so earnest that Abner smiled, patted his shoulder and said, 'Well, maybe one

32

of the others'll have seen those boys.'

He went back to the top stair and paused there to glance in the direction of Whittier's closed room then went slowly and thoughtfully down.

Outside, the night was pleasant. There was no moon but there were a myriad of stars. It was pleasantly warm, too, but then in New Mexico in summertime it usually was warm. In fact, later on it would be downright uncomfortably hot.

He left the boarding house by way of the dimly-lighted rear kitchen, almost broke his neck over a big garbage tin someone had left directly beyond the doorway, and leaned upon a porch-upright to groan and swear and massage a bruised shin.

Then he went out to the horse shed, which hadn't had a horse in it to Abner's knowledge in six or seven years, since the boarding house had stopped taking in transients and had accepted only permanent residents, and found what he had half-expected might be out there. A handsome big strong bay horse eating from a cribbed old manger, wearing his saddle and having his bridle hanging from the saddlehorn.

He felt his way around, examined the horse and the saddle, saw where a little hay and grain had been stored, saw where there had for a time been a second horse, and finally stepped back into the darker shadows near the rear of the old shed, and composed himself for a comfortable wait.

Perhaps as a result of his recent visit upstairs his wait was not very long. He heard someone hastening across through the weeds long before they entered the horse shed. He recognised the store-clerk the moment the man stepped inside lugging his bedroll under his left arm while he had his bulging saddlebags slung carelessly over his right shoulder.

Abner allowed the man to put down the bedroll and move to first tie the saddlebags aft of the cantle before bridling the horse. When the clerk had both arms upraised across the near-rump of the bay, Abner unshipped his Colt and said, 'Don't move. Keep your arms up there like that, Mister Whittier!'

The clerk kicked both feet from beneath himself and as he fell he drew and twisted.

Abner fired at the faint-seen shadowy silhouette of a man's upper carcass. The clerk also fired, but he was a yard wide, and in all probability he did not really know where Abner was.

The sheriff's second gunshot sent the bay horse charging out of the shed with a broken halter dangling on his head.

That time there was no return shot. The clerk was lying face down and arms upflung along the earthen floor.

Abner waited for the echoes to die away, then he stepped over, kicked the loose

34

revolver away, leaned and flung the clerk over at the same time shoving his cocked sixgun at the man's head.

The clerk's wide-open eyes stared straight up. That second shot had caught the man slightly higher than in the centre of the forehead.

Abner stepped around to see where that horse had gone with the saddlebags on his back.

CHAPTER FOUR

SOMETHING TO BE DONE

Carey Brookshire said, 'Old Lewis is fit to be tied. He told me and some other fellers that when you give him back half that bank money you wouldn't say a word to him. He's dyin' to know how you figured it was that store-clerk.'

Abner shrugged. 'I didn't know it was him, I just thought it darned well might be, and when he walked into the horse-shed, hell, I was just running a bluff to scare him out if he was . . . Some bluff; that crazy son of a bitch dropped down and started shooting. But you don't have to tell Lewis that. Let him think I'm Sherlock Holmes.'

Brookshire was still as nonplussed as everyone else was around town; the ones that were either awakened by the gun shots or had not yet gone to bed and who rushed forth to see what all the commotion was about. Brookshire was one of the latter. He said, 'What about the other one, Abner?'

The best answer to this question was the answer Abner gave. 'I don't know any more about him than you do. I was hoping Whittier would be able to tell me something.'

'Not unless you want to go down where it's awful hot,' muttered the blacksmith. 'Hell! if the other one hears about Whittier being found out and shot he'll fly the coop and keep flying. The bank'll never get the other half of the money back.'

'Half is more'n John Lewis expected to get back,' rebutted the sheriff, and yawned. It had been a long day.

'You got any suspicions?' asked the blacksmith. 'I mean; that other one was also from around here close, was he?'

Abner was certain that the other one had never before in his life been even close to Bellsville. 'The other one came from out of the territory.' He yawned and Carey Brookshire took the hint.

'I'll see you in the morning,' he said, and left Abner at the jailhouse alone, but not for long. The liveryman walked in acting as though it wasn't getting on close to midnight, and said, 'I've went and impounded that dead man's horse, Abner, and his outfit. You know that's

36

one hell of a nice bay horse. If no one puts in a claim for him before the time runs out, by golly I think I'll buy him.'

'You do that,' stated the sheriff, and eased his caller to the door and out it into the cooling night. 'See you in the morning, Lester.'

This time Abner did not return inside except for the one brief moment that was required to blow down the mantle of his desk-lamp.

He almost made it to the boarding house but the banker John Lewis caught him out front of Clement Bowie's harness works with a big broad smile and his outstretched hand. Evidently banker Lewis had decided to act as though Sheriff Wright hadn't cut him off when he'd returned that loot from the outlaw's saddlebags.

But Abner felt the same and let it show when he barely touched Lewis's hand by way of a shake, then said, 'I'm on my way home to bed, Mister Lewis. See you in the—'

'Abner, you deserve to hear my apology,' exclaimed the banker. 'I was unnecessarily rough on you, accusing you of not doing enough and all, saying I'd fetch in the army and the U.S. Marshal. Abner, you deserve the thanks not only of the bank and its depositors, but of the entire community.'

Abner's impatience came up very quickly. 'Why don't you go tell all this bullcrap to someone who might like to hear it, Mister

Lewis?' he asked, and turned on his heel.

The boarding house was also alight, both upstairs and downstairs. Abner avoided all additional contact by going down alongside the old building to his private doorway. Inside, he did not bother lighting a lamp. He had been dressing and undressing the same carcass for over thirty years; he didn't need any light to do it by.

He dropped into bed, closed his eyes, saw that black stealthy silhouette again, and opened his eyes. No one who was in his right mind slept or ate well after killing a fellow human being. Not even when the fellow human being was as worthless and treacherous as that store-clerk had been.

He sat on the edge of the bed and made a cigarette, smoked it slowly, and by the time he was down to the butt and crushed the thing out, he could finally lie back and almost immediately go to sleep.

He was still sleeping the following morning when the sun came through a window and hit him across the face. He groaned and sat up to look wetly around. He had not meant to sleep past dawn.

The world he awakened to was fresh and clean with a summer-scent of sumac and sage and new-day warmth. He rolled out, dressed and went out to the wash-house to make himself presentable and afterwards used the back-alley to walk down past the jailhouse where he did not even hesitate, to go as far as the livery barn.

Lester was down there giving his dayman instructions and saw the sheriff come in from out back. Lester waited, watching Sheriff Wright before he went over to speak to him, and at the last moment a sixth sense warned the liveryman, so he simply went up as far as his little cubbyhole of an office and stood around out front, up there, watching. Some men he knew from a long lifetime of experience did not appreciate being accosted either carefully or heartily first thing in the morning. Clearly, judging from the look on Abner Wright's face this morning, he did not want to be bothered.

The dayman went over to lend a hand and got growled at for his troubles. Lester nodded as though this were something he would have anticipated and the dayman veered off, giving Abner a wide berth.

The horse, fortunately, had been fed two hours earlier, he was as full as a tick and was ready for exercise so he stood as docilely as a lamb while Abner rigged him out, then led him into the alley and swung aboard.

Lester walked back there to stand and watch as Sheriff Wright headed up the alleyway. The dayman came over and leaned on his manure-fork as he said, 'He's went and strapped the carbine-boot to the saddle just like he looked when he came in last evening.

I'd say he was going somewhere for a fact.'

The liveryman looked disdainfully around. Anyone who saddled, bridled, and stepped up into the middle of his damned horse was obviously going somewhere, and Lester was disgusted to his bone-marrow to hear anyone make such a ridiculous statement.

The day hostler smiled. 'Be headin' for Outlaw Town maybe. You figure? Well; around town yestiddy there was plenty of talk that if he didn't go up there and clean out that nest of rattlers somebody would have to, and I heard at the saloon that Mister Lewis from the bank had said he'd hire a bunch of gunfighters, if he had to, and send them up there. Or maybe even get the army to ride up there with cannons and all.'

Lester said, 'Oh, for Chris'sake,' and turned irritably to stamp back up through his barn to the office. He had never heard such a silly lot of talk in his life; Sheriff Wright didn't have to be going any place special just because he rode with a carbine slung under his *rosadero*; lots of men ride with carbines on their saddles, and moreover anyone in their right mind would know that Sheriff Wright wasn't insane enough, or simple-minded enough, to try and ride up through those lousy mountains to Outlaw Town all by himself.

Several other people saw Abner pass up out of town northbound by way of the back alley and they didn't think much of it either.

Primarily because Abner rode out of town quite a bit, especially this pleasant time of year, and partly because, as Lester had said, they believed a man would have to be crazy as a pet 'coon to head for Outlaw Town by himself.

Maybe they were right.

One thing was abundantly clear; a person could go around the Bellsville countryside for a long while asking if someone would do that, and all he'd get would be negative answers.

On the other hand if a person were indeed heading up into the mountains he could not have picked a finer day for it. Of course riding out of Bellsville an hour or two earlier would have been preferable because it would have put Abner across those distant foothills and into the real mountains with enough daylight left to have a fair start towards his destination, come morning.

But if a man overslept there was nothing much he could do to reverse that condition, except perhaps keep on riding when he might normally have called it quits for the day.

As for his goal, he thought he knew approximately where it was, but that was a little like talking about that proverbial needle in the haystack. Those were huge mountains, miles deep and miles wide. There could have been ten villages up in there without folks knowing exactly where they were.

But he rode confidently. If he didn't find

them, they would find him, and either way, while his reception might be cool at the best, and downright unpleasant at its worst, that was the chance he'd have to take. He preferred it to waiting until a big posse of armed townsmen and rangemen could be got together to ride up in there with him; that kind of an invasion could only result in either sniping or a pitched battle, and while, as many people had been saying over the years, this was what was needed to clean out the mountains, Abner was unconvinced for a very simple reason : He had never been up there before, had no idea what the town was like nor its inhabitants, and was simply averse to the use of overwhelming gunpower just for the sake of force.

He had no intention of being shot out of the saddle, either. He had heard how the residents of Outlaw Town used their little green stones to guide people in, and how they used them to keep people out, and along with this system of protection he had also been told that they kept scouts or sentries posted on the higher lowland ridges, and beside all the trails leading to the town.

He did not intend to skulk up and spy on the town like an Indian and he did not mean to go whistling up the trail to be deliberately captured. His idea was to go up as far as he thought he had ought to go, and from there on perhaps try to contact at least one resident of the town. He needed a sponsor one way or another; either to sponsor him as a friend or to sponsor him as a suspicious character, but at least he needed someone to get him into the town without being shot at.

He rode along without speculating much on how he would depart from Outlaw Town. They would know who he was within an hour or less of the time he arrived there, he had no illusions about that, and planning beyond his arrival there did not strike him as being very worthwhile. A man lived his life from day to day, at best and at worst.

There was also the possibility that men he had either jailed, turned over to the judicial authorities to be sentenced to prison, or men he had whipped for being troublesome in Bellsville might be up there. He would no doubt have plenty of enmity on all sides without those people too.

Maybe it was crazy, what he was doing, but by the time he passed through the foothills and was heading over a game-trail into the more rugged uplands country it was in his opinion too late to go back, even if he'd felt like going back, which he didn't.

The horse was strong, the weather continued warm even into late afternoon, and the mountains were more inviting and interesting the farther into them he rode.

He knew most of the trail he would pass over during his initial penetration of the mountains. He knew for example where the

Cutlass Cattle Company had one of its line-cabins a mile or so up through the initial area of meadows, glens and dark forests, and he also knew where there was a peeled-pole big corral made many years earlier by some of the first stockmen to come into the country.

He had hunted up through these mountains each autumn since coming to Durham County, but it was unlikely that anyone he knew had ever gone as far back through the mountains as he was going to travel this time.

After about mid-afternoon tomorrow he would be out of the territory he knew and he would also be out of the territory he had heard the stockmen talk of when they'd gone cattle-gathering in the fall of the year, and afterwards congregated in town to talk about it.

The town, he thought, was another twenty or maybe even thirty miles onward, perhaps over against the final high-rising area which seemed to be flat and rather extensive at the base of the final high rims.

That was a guess. 'Hell,' he told the indifferent horse, 'Everything we're doing is a guess. For all I know their lousy town could be no more'n ten miles onward and we'll ride up into the middle of 'em before we even suspect it.'

He didn't really believe that and his horse was concerned with finding the place where they would spend the night so he could go foraging. He was hungry again by late afternoon.

They came to the line-camp cabin at roughly the same time the shadows of forest and mountain closed in around the lower elevations.

He off-saddled, washed the horse's back at the creek, hobbled him and watched him go hopping away into the small lush meadow out behind the cabin where Cutlass Cattle Company saddle stock had been grazing for more than twenty-five years each time Cutlass cowboys came up here hunting Cutlass livestock.

The cabin was clean and orderly. There was food in two large wooden boxes suspended from the log rafters by wire, so that rodents and raccoons and porcupines could not get the tins and boxes.

The cabin was one room in size, made of squared fir logs notched perfectly at each corner. There was an iron wood-stove and three wall-bunks. There was even kindling wood in the woodbox, and anyone using the facility was expected to leave it as they had found it, which meant re-filling the woodbox, and sweeping out, the implements for which were hanging from pegs on the wall.

Abner got comfortable, built a nice fire, ate supper, then banked his fire to keep the cabin warm throughout the night and bedded down. It was in some ways better than bedding down in a hotel in some strange town. At least a bunch of noisy cowboys whooping it up as they raced out of town didn't interrupt a man's rest.

CHAPTER FIVE

RIDING A PARTICULAR RIDGE

A big cougar screamed though, in the middle of the night, and that was enough to wake a man out of a sound sleep with his hair standing on end.

Abner took his carbine, pulled on his britches and boots and went out back to see if the horse was upset. There was a sickle moon and a host of white-lighted stars to brighten the meadow.

His horse was standing out there as erect as a stone carving peering steadily in the direction from which that scream had come. The horse was poised for flight, hobbles or not.

Abner spoke to him then walked on across the meadow not especially looking for the cougar but in order to spread his man-scent around, then he made a circuitous stroll which ended up back at the line-shack where he went inside, leaned the carbine beside the door, and went back to bed.

Morning arrived without there having been additional interruptions. Abner had a little food in his saddlebags. He carried flat tins, enough for a couple of very scanty meals, all the time. Now, he made his skimpy breakfast without borrowing any Cutlass Cattle Company supplies, and later went back to the meadow where his horse was dozing, sleek and full and perfectly willing to go right on sleeping.

He was on the trail ahead of daylight, but in the mountains the sun seldom appeared at the same time on different days. The higher a man rode the earlier he met dawn, the lower he rode into meadows and ravines, the later he met dawn. For Abner Wright the new daylight did not arrive until he had crested a wide, forested grassy ridge and was passing down the far side of it where there was more grass and less timber. There, sunlight had already melted away the dew and a small band of does with their fawns were already finishing their morning browsing. They did not see Abner and his horse until he was less than a hundred yards off, and called softly, good-naturedly, to them, then they swung heads which seemed swivelled on rubber necks, watched a moment, then fled all in a frantic rush.

He shook his head. If he'd been a hunter in need of camp-meat he could have shot down at least two of them without difficulty.

There was a broad trail across the meadow where those deer had been. It looked as though it had been made by horsemen but, of course, it hadn't, it had been made by high-country elk. He followed it because it went approximately in the direction he wanted to ride, and later, when it veered left down into the lush bottoms of a wide, green ravine he turned off and searched for another trail heading north-west. He did not find one from this point onward but as it happened the country was not too wooded for pleasant travel so he had no difficulty. In fact, this country he was now crossing through was very pleasant. There was abundant feed, a number of little creeks running southward, and plenty of timbered areas for shade and shelter. It was good cattle-territory except for one thing—that foraging cougar last night had not been looking for a man or a man's horse, he had been looking for something less likely to be dangerous to kill, and there were also bears up through here, brown and black ones, as well as deadly packs of wolves. Someday, Abner told the horse, as they went comfortably along, someone would come up in here, thin out the predators, and run cattle up here. It was beautiful country, and peacefully secluded.

He was familiar with parts of it. In fact he paused in one little brush-encircled meadow where, on a windy day one time, he had killed a big fat three-year-old buck deer.

But as the day wore along he passed gradually out of the territory where he had hunted down the years and began looking upon slopes and ridges and down into broad, wide little shallow meadows and parks he had never seen before. By mid-afternoon it was all entirely strange to him.

Where he nooned was overlooking a game trail and before he left a band of deer had strolled along in communal order, entirely unsuspecting. Later, he saw them enter a big lush meadow and fan out as though this were their normal habitat. He was upon an eastern slope angling around it, and the deer did not see him up there.

The territory began to turn rough only near the end of his first full day in the mountains, and even then, if he had not persevered steadily ahead he would have remained in the beautifully open and rolling territory.

There was heat everywhere except among the spits of forest he passed through, and in those places it was cool and gloomy and anciently padded with layers of pine and fir needles. Even a shod horse could pass through those places without making a sound.

Once, because of this silence, he was able to watch a bitch wolf and her four pups playing roughly near a sidehill den. The pups were like tawny fur-balls. They rolled into her at fulltilt and when she would grab one with her teeth he would spit and growl and act like a spoiled two-legged child. As a matter of fact they did have much in common; many wolf-mothers did not discipline their offspring either.

He whistled to let the bitch know he was crossing through and in a twinkling she had hurled her pups unceremoniously into the den and had disappeared down there after them. In five seconds there was no indication that any animals had ever played in the grass along their private ridge.

The farther Abner rode the more it struck him that human travel through at least this part of the mountains had never been more than very rare. Otherwise the animals would have left, or, the ones who hadn't left would have been much more alert than the animals he had encountered so far, and what all this boiled down to, clearly, was that he was nowhere near Outlaw Town, and that neither was he using any of the routes knowledgeable fugitives used to reach Outlaw Town.

He was less discouraged than he was inclined to alter course. He decided to go over closer to the coachroad, easterly. Maybe that would prove to be the wrong direction too, but he only had a pair of them to choose from, east and west, and he might as well tackle one as the other.

But by the time he got over easterly far enough to be able to see the stageroad it was getting too dark to see it. However, he did find one interesting item. He was working his way up near the top out of a gravelly, wind-swept ledge when he found a freshly cast, badly worn-down horseshoe. It was still shiny. He swung down to retrieve it, and to study it, then he studied the trail he was using and located faint impressions of a ridden animal also heading up the slope towards that gravelly ridge.

A wise man might have turned around and retreated, except that if there was someone up ahead, perhaps overhead, he could turn and glance down—and instantly catch the sight of movement.

Abner pocketed the shoe and started forward, leading his horse from here on. It was steep, the horse had been working hard all day on nothing but washy meadow-grass, and anyway a little exercise was good for a man.

It required another half-hour to reach the gravelly ridge by which time it was getting along towards full dusk. He made his approach very carefully, but there was no one up there, and although he looked carefully for the signs, there was no indication that the horse with three shod hooves had been up there.

Abner was not a good tracker, obviously, since there was no other place for that unknown horseman to go once he started up. But knowing he was not good at tracking helped a lot; he found a place among some warped and twisted junipers to leave the horse, took the carbine and crept back out along the rim, which was too gravelly and wind-scourged for there to be much undergrowth, and which was fairly broad and long. In fact, out where the ridge ended against a somewhat abrupt drop-off of a slope which headed almost directly eastward in the direction of the stageroad, there were several tall fir trees which had been protected from winter rawness because they'd started growing from just below the easterly ridge. From among those trees a man had a good view of a lot of country, mostly eastward, but also southward down where the roadway meandered to the range, where it flattened out and ran arrow-straight all the way to Bellsville, and northward, where it came painstakingly over through a low notch in the skyline. Up there the visibility from the tree-sheltered peak had all the most distant slopes well in view, in daylight, but when Abner worked his way soundlessly out to the edge of those trees it was too dark to see much of anything, although the stageroad was eerily visible because it was grey-white and seemingly endless the way it came out of the most northerly gloom and went hastening southward out into more shrouding gloom.

Abner paused in shelter to consider. Somewhere on this plateau there was another mounted man. If he wasn't still up here, then, as fresh as that old cast shoe was, he could not be much farther down that eastern drop-off. If he had a lick of sense he wouldn't try to navigate that drop-off in the deceptively murderous dusk, either. It would be dangerous enough for a mounted man in broad daylight.

Abner picked up the pleasant scent of tobacco smoke and smiled to himself. Since he had been unable to see the stranger when the light had been adequate, and since he had been unable to see his horse-tracks either, but the man was somewhere out through that little spit of trees somewhere, perhaps sitting there smoking in blissful ignorance as he went about making his camp for the night, one thing was a lead-pipe cinch; there was a stranger in among the trees!

Abner enjoyed the tobacco-scent. It made him want also to light up. Instead he knelt to remove his spurs and shove each spur into a rear trouser pocket, pick up the carbine and start onward. He was careful where he stepped, but once he got in among the tall trees he did not worry much about being heard by the stranger. He worried a little about the stranger's horse detecting his scent though.

There were never any guarantees in a dangerous situation. A man did the best he knew to do, and went ahead as prudently and carefully as he could, otherwise he kept his gun in hand, and was prepared to at least get off a good second shot.

But it never came to that. Abner saw the horse finally, grazing and edging its way out along the drop-off, or at least edging perilously close to the drop-off. He was not hobbled but he was dragging a lass rope made fast by one half of a set of hobbles to the animal's left ankle. He was a big seal-brown horse and in the gloom looked younger than he probaby was, but he was rawboned and powerful, exactly the kind of a horse a man would want in mountainous country, where neither appearance nor speed meant anything.

Abner could have worked his way around to get between the horse and the trees along the road-side of the ridge but he elected not to because of the degree of open country where he would be exposed. Whether he was dealing with an outlaw or just a traveller made no difference under these circumstances; no one reacted amiably to being stalked in the night up through a part of the country which was notorious for being liable to have outlaws anywhere in it.

But he had stood back there where he'd first spied the horse long enough to arrive at some tentative conclusions. Granted, they arose from the fact that he was by trade a lawman, nevertheless the same thoughts might have arrived eventually to anyone else who had come up here and had found someone out there upon the edge of the rim where he was overlooking the stageroad. The stranger did not have to camp out there; in fact he had passed a number of much better places to camp. But if his intention was to spy on the road until he saw a stage passing down-country from the higher areas, with the idea in mind of descending to the westerly edge of the road in plenty of time to set up a robber's ambush, why then where the man now was had to be the best place around.

Any range-rider who was up there where Abner was, would have suspected something like this, unless he was just plain simple in the head.

Abner sighed and started down through the trees, one careful step at a time.

He did not see a campfire and did not expect to see one. No outlaw camping upon a promontory would ever light a fire even to make his evening coffee by. By the time Abner got into the thickest and darkest part of those trees he could hear a man moving around out yonder near the drop-off, out where the trees actually grew up from below the rim.

The seal-brown horse was no longer in view. He had either stepped down over the drop-off or he had gone back along the north-westerly side of the promontory. Abner hoped for his sake he hadn't tried to navigate that abrupt drop-off in the dark with that dragging lass-rope on his leg.

Someone out through the trees made a few hard knocking sounds, then mouthed a harmonica. The music was lilting and not very loud. Abner did not know the song but he liked it and he also liked the stranger's ability to play music, but best of all the new sound was just loud enough to allow Abner to pass across the last intervening fifteen or twenty yards and halt beside a huge old rough-baked red fir with the squatting stranger in plain sight.

The man was thick and massive, built like a bear, and nearly as shaggy-headed as one. He looked to Abner as though he hadn't been near a town in months. Not only did his wavy dark hair reach to his shoulders but his beard was untrimmed and as shaggy as the side of a shedding buffalo.

The man's hat was lying in the pine-needles at his side. There was also a Winchester lying there, and in plain sight where the man sat upon a rotting old tree stump, was the bone-handle of a boot-knife showing out of the stranger's boot-top.

He looked like one of those old-time buffalo hunters or Indian-fighters, but his spurs were from Mexico with big rowels, and his bedroll and lariat and saddlebags were those of a rangeman.

Abner finally knew one of the songs the stranger was playing. Evidently it had a significance to the stranger because before putting his heart into the music, he slapped the harmonica upon a trouser-leg to clear it of excess moisture. Then he leaned forward concentrating upon his playing. He had music rising up through the lonely and distant night that would have tugged at the heartstrings of anyone, and finally, as he reared back and allowed the finale to reach a poignant *crescendo*, he saw the man standing beside the fir-tree with his Winchester held across his body two-handed, aimed squarely at him.

Still, the big, hairy man finished his music, did not cut it short by so much as one chord, and afterwards when he lowered the mouth-harp and tapped it against his leg again, he smiled a little through all that facial hair, eyeing Abner, as he said, 'Well sir, *amigo*, I'm obliged for the audience. Usually it's coyotes and magpies and camp-robbers. Don't ordinarily get people to listen. Mainly, I expect, because I don't play where there are people.'

Abner watched the burly older man pocket his harmonica and gently lower his right hand. Abner wig-wagged his carbine and the big man sighed and gently moved his right hand back away from the saw-handle grip of his holstered Colt. He smiled. 'Mister, if you're the law or if you ain't, to me it's pretty much all the same. I got reason not to want to go along with you.'

'And I got reason for not taking you along with me,' answered Abner, letting the Winchester's barrel droop a little. 'If you're waiting for a stage, you should have been up here a lot earlier in the day.'

The burly man shrugged. 'Don't make it today, why then I'll make it tomorrow. When you get my age a day more or less don't make much difference.' He pointed. 'There's elk jerky and a canteen of good branch-water if you're hungry, friend, and I'll pass you my word not to try and shoot you while you're eatin' supper. That's not at all a tidy thing for folks to do, is it?'

The burly man grinned and Abner could not hold back a desire to return the grin as he said, 'Sure wouldn't be a tidy thing to do.'

But he did not accept the stranger's invitation.

CHAPTER SIX

SUNDAY

The thickly-made older man's name was Porter Sunday, and when he said that, he cocked an eye at Abner as though he did not expect to be believed, and said, 'Well, I also been called Tom Jones and Tom Smith,' then he smiled again. He seemed to smile broadly and readily without much encouragement. He had small blue eyes made to look even smaller in their setting among all his full whiskers.

Until he stood up Abner had had some notion that he was not a very tall man, but evidently that was because of his thickness when he was sitting. When he rose he was easily six feet tall, an inch or two taller than Abner, and he was downright massive in build. He was one of those men who never had to work hard at avoiding trouble; all Porter Sunday would normally have to do would be to stand up—and smile—and clearly he had done it often. He, in fact, did it now; he arose, smiled at Abner and acted as though Abner did not have his carbine aimed at him as he stepped to the careless pile of horse-gear and rummaged for several pieces of peppery jerky which he chewed upon thoughtfully as he studied Abner.

It was easy to understand people underestimating that smiling big bear of a man. He did not look harmless at all but he always looked friendly, and that was one of his advantages. Abner had seen this kind of a man before. Until a person knew the exact degree of their treachery, they were more deadly and potentially dangerous than a professional gunman.

Porter Sunday said, 'Well, sir, friend, here we are—standing around lookin' at one another, and don't seem likely we'll want to go on doin' this all night, so maybe you won't mind if I fetch out my blankets and bed down.' Porter Sunday looked around with what Abner thought was exaggerated interest. 'Where's your horse,' he asked Abner, 'and your bedroll and whatnots?' He rolled his eyes. 'Brother, if you're travellin' in just what you're standin' up in right now, that'll mean you got a posse right behind you.'

Abner shook his head. 'No posse. I hid my

horse back a ways when I found this.' He pitched the worn-out cast shoe to Porter Sunday. The bearded man caught the shoe and held it close to study it for a long while, then he said, 'Off my horse?'

'Off the only other horse to come the trail ahead of me,' stated Abner.

The older man's eyes narrowed in a scowl and he turned to look through the trees in the direction his horse had taken. 'Gawddamn,' he said with feeling. 'Now what'n'ell am I supposed to do? Is there a place anywhere around where I can get a new shoe put on him?'

'About fifteen, eighteen miles southward down that stageroad,' replied Abner. 'Place called Bellsville. Mister Sunday; you sure had it coming. That darned shoe isn't much thicker'n paper. The nail head's been worn down for days. Most men look after their horse's shoes better than that.'

Porter Sunday grimaced. 'Friend, I don't ride through many towns. I got my reasons— besides from not liking towns. I usually do my own shoeing at a ranch or cow-camp, and lately we just haven't come onto any.' Porter Sunday's little eyes settled intently upon Abner. 'Where is your horse; why don't you go fetch him back to camp so's he can graze around here instead of standin' half the night tethered to a tree?'

'Because I don't like the idea of turning my

back on you,' replied Abner, and the bearded man threw back his head and roared with laughter. He had a set of teeth to chew through iron with and a powerful neck the size of an oak tree. When he'd finished laughing and lowered his head he said, 'Sonny, I ain't going to back-shoot you. In fact I was thinkin' that between the pair of us we could stop the stage that'll likely come down that pike in the morning, and be out of this country in nothing flat. It always works better with two fellers than with one.'

'Where,' asked Abner, 'out of this country?' and the big older man threw his arms wide in an open gesture. 'Anywhere,' he said. 'In any direction.'

Abner wondered. 'Where are you from?' he asked.

'Down through the Chiricahuas near the Mex border,' replied the bearded man. 'Mister, I been an outlaw all my life. Well; maybe except for four years when I was married. But right after that I come back to it. I'm going onto fifty-two this autumn. I worked in cow-camps, logging-camps, drove coaches and drove cattle, but for a decent livin' son, you can't do better'n steal a little.'

Porter Sunday went back to his tree-stump and sat down eyeing Abner. 'And you—you been a cowboy,' he said. 'Well, sir, that's a healthy life for a fact, but let me tell you it's healthier and the pay's better when you stop coaches and maybe now and then raid an outlying ranch when no one's to home. And keep moving, Mister, keep moving. I don't believe they even got any decent posters out on me in the last six, eight years; lousy lawmen wouldn't know enough to lay hands on me . . . Mister, you got a name?'

'Abner.'

'That's all? Are you plain Abner or maybe Mister Abner?'

'Plain Abner. Mister Sunday, have you ever been up through these mountains before?'

'No, sir, I never have. I been over east forty or so miles, though, and I been down south a hunnert or so miles quite a lot. Abner, I know that border country better'n I know the back of my own hand.'

'Did you ever hear of a place up in these mountains called Outlaw Town?' asked Abner, and watched the other man's face for the reaction which never showed there.

'Hey, Abner—do you believe that cock 'n' bull yarn? I heard it before, sure. A regular town owned and run by fugitives and renegades. Abner, how old are you? You don't look young enough to believe a story like that.'

Abner smiled. 'It's up there, Mister Sunday.'

The professional outlaw sat back staring at Abner. 'You're crazy,' he finally said with frank candour. 'There's no such place.'

'There *is* such a place. It's back against the northward mountains. You don't have to believe it if you don't want to, but there is such a place. A town run by outlaws.'

'You want to know what I think, Abner?'

'Not especially, since you've already told me anyway.'

'. . . Is that where you're heading, by any chance?' asked Porter Sunday, and Abner inclined his head. Porter Sunday sat back and stared.

'You're not kidding me nor lyin' to old Port, nor makin' fun of me, Abner?'

'Like I said, it's back there. You can go ahead and raid the stage in the morning by yourself. The only reason I stalked you was to have a look. I didn't want to pick up a lawman on my trail while I was heading for Outlaw Town.' Abner lowered the carbine and leaned upon it eyeing the older man. 'Porter; pitch that sixgun over into the grass. And the boot-knife. And kick that Winchester plumb away too.'

Sunday stared, then he guessed why these orders had been given and leaned with a grunt to obey. He said, 'Oh hell! do I really look that darned treacherous, that I'd shoot you in the back when you walked away from here?'

'Yeah. Quit talkin' and throw the guns away.'

Sunday obeyed. He winced when his flung Colt struck a rock and spun around as it landed. 'Gawddamned country anyway,' he moaned. 'Looks soft with pine needles and has

63

rocks under them.' He looked over at Abner. 'Listen; we could raid that coach, then if you still was of a mind to, we could go together and hunt up this supposed town run by fugitives.'

Abner grinned. 'Thanks,' he said. 'Good luck, Port. And if you don't want to die right here on this lousy ridge, don't get off that stump until I'm plumb gone, because if I hear a sound I'm going to start shooting.'

'You're not real hospitable,' muttered the burly man, and dug out his harmonica. 'I'll keep playin' while you're walking away, and that'll let you know where I am all the while.'

Abner was agreeable. 'Play,' he said, as he backed around the fir tree he had been leaning upon and waited until the music began before continuing to withdraw back along the ridge in the direction of the area where he had left his horse.

He could still hear that harmonica when he untied the horse, turned and led it over to the uphill trail, and started down.

The idea of stopping Sunday from ambushing the morning stage had been strongly in his mind until he reflected that not only would he then have to go back to Bellsville, again, this time with a prisoner, but even if he did nothing to stop the robbery it was improbable that Porter Sunday would get much since there were no bullion stages on the Bellsville run, and hadn't been since the mines had closed down over the mountains ten years or so earlier.

He would get some money from the stage crew and the passengers. When Abner got back he would be able to give more information on Porter Sunday than anyone else had apparently ever given on him. Sunday would be caught when all that information plus a likeness would be put upon a wanted dodger and circulated throughout the territory. That was how it worked, and usually it worked very well.

He got down to the lower territory again, and continued to lead his horse. He did this for no particular reason except that on a downhill slope or on level ground he did not mind walking.

He made several cutbacks, and those were also accomplished for no particular reason because no one, not even a mountain-outlaw whose face resembled the back-end of a bear, could track him in the night.

It was the horse who picked their nightcamp this time. He either heard running water or smelled it and tugged gently. Abner allowed himself to be led into a small glade, perhaps two acres in size, where a sweet-water creek coming down across rocks in the middle distance, sliced through a corner of the grassland. It was not as dark in this place as it had been back upon the slope leading down from the gravelly ridge, but neither was it altogether clear and bright because the sun was gone and there were shadows all around. The stars were faintly visible but evidently that little moon left over from the previous night would not be showing for a while yet.

Abner off-saddled, settled his horse for the night, made up a summer-pallet of horsesweat-scented saddleblanket, grass and armloads of needles, and bedded down without eating. He did not even have a smoke before kicking out of his boots and bedding down.

Sleep was never a problem for Abner Wright, not even upon a damp saddleblanket under a covering of grass and pine needles. Hunger was never very much of a problem to him either. He was a philosophical man, whether he realised it or not; if he could sleep in a bed he was pleased, if he could eat well before bedding down, he was pleased too, but if neither of these things were immediately available when it came time to do one or the other, he was not especially inconvenienced. He accepted life as it came; had learned long ago to do that, and perhaps as a result of this uniquely Wright outlook, when he thought it was probably time to strike out again he rolled up out of his grass and needles and looked around as he always did, for the horse.

Porter Sunday was sitting upon Abner's saddle whittling on strips of jerky with that wicked-bladed boot-knife. He looked over, nodded, and returned to his whittling. When he had enough strips he dropped them into a tiny dented, dirty pan which was already two-thirds full of creek water, and put the pan atop some stones he'd created a fire-ring out of, then got down on all fours looking more than ever bear-like, and blew gently upon some shavings atop pine needles inside the fire-ring. As soon as smoke curled upwards Porter rocked back on powerful haunches and tugged at his beard watching the fire as he said, 'Mister Abner; remind me sometime to tell you how me and Al Sieber tracked Naná and Geronimo right into their soogans one time, and routed them out with squaws screeching like cougars.'

He blew a big breath, rubbed his hands together and turned. 'Abner, I got to see a town run by outlaws. I don't believe it exists. It's just impossible. But you're not a lyin' sort of man and by gawd if you believe it's up here somewhere, then old Port wants to go along and see it too. And if it ain't back there, Abner, old Port is going to bust half your ribs for makin' a fool out of him.' Porter Sunday held up a huge paw. 'Don't reach for the Colt.' He smiled showing those perfect, powerful white teeth again. 'I unloaded it before sunup. Abner, roll out and go wash at the creek. I didn't, but then I can't abide real cold water. But you're younger. I'll have breakfas' ready when you get back.'

Abner had not opened his mouth. He scratched a little, looked for his horse and saw two grazing horses, then yawned, spat aside and gazed at Porter Sunday's formidable profile. He had never in his life travelled with a man as hairy as Sunday, and in fact he had never actually known a man that hairy. Porter's hat just barely managed to stay up there atop that incredible mass of wavy, shoulder-length hair. In a place like Bellsville only one thing would keep a man like Sunday out of a fight every night at the saloon. His size.

Abner said, 'I don't want you along when I ride up to Outlaw Town. No offence, Mister Sunday, but I think a man coming in by himself would be more welcome.'

Sunday shook his hairy head. 'Nope. If this town is really run by other wanted men, they'll like the notion of two more hands joining them. We'll ride up there together . . . But I still think it's a damned mirage; a big story someone told you and because you're gullible you—'

'I know it's back there!' exclaimed Abner, rolling out. Porter Sunday had a way of irritating Abner, and not just because Abner was always ready to be irritable first thing in the morning. Last night he'd also irritated him.

Sunday turned and watched Abner stalk off in the direction of the creek. He shook his head ruefully and spat amber into their breakfast fire. The hell of it was, being unable to go openly in search of companionship when a man was travelling, he had to accept what the good Lord set down near him and it usually was not anything he'd voluntarily select. This young cowboy was a good man; Port Sunday had never in his troubled life misjudged another man. If he had by now he would have been dead. But sometimes being a good man wasn't as nice as having a feller along who could also make a little music and who could swap lies with a straight face, and who could rob a coach wearing a smile behind his neckerchief. But, the way things worked out, more often than not a man had to take what was sent his way.

And a lawman at that.

Porter lifted the badge from his shirt-pocket, eyed it again and dropped it back into the pocket. One of the advantages of being an old border hand was that a man could pick someone's pockets while they were snoring their damned head off, and occasionally come up with something very interesting.

A damned lawman. Porter would have been willing to bet a good horse Abner was on the run. Last night, of course it had been dark and all, but Porter did not misjudge men, and last night that blasted lawman had stood right there looking Port squarely in the eye talking about robbing the morning stage.

Of course, not all lawmen were above turning a little handy profit when there was no danger to them involved. Maybe that was it.

Abner's groans from the ice-water creek came back to Potter. Sunday nodded his head; anyone who would wash in water like that deserved anything that befell them!

CHAPTER SEVEN

A STONE

Abner dried off on his shirt-tail over at the creek and weighed the advantages against the disadvantages of having Porter Sunday with him. It was easy to imagine reasons for not having Porter ride along, but the longer he dwelt upon the notion the more it occurred to him that Porter might be useful. Abner knew about what he was riding into; he was known in Outlaw Town. Perhaps having an old border outlaw with him when he rode in, back there, would register in his favour.

As he shrugged into his shirt and turned to go back he decided there was not going to be very much he could do about it; Sunday had decided he was going to ride along, and he had unloaded Abner's sixgun as part of his argument. For a while, then, Abner would be saddled with the bearded man, and actually, the advantage versus the disadvantage was very slight. So slight in fact that when he strode back he hadn't really come to a decision. At least not a wholehearted one.

Porter had divided the breakfast stew of pepper-cured jerky with scrupulous honesty and had put Abner's tin dish over where he sat down. 'I been out of coffee for weeks,' he told Abner. 'I'm almost weaned off it.' He grinned through all that hair. 'Of course, if I was to find any I'd maybe kill a man to get it.'

The stew was not bad. It was better than Abner would have had if Porter Sunday hadn't arrived.

Porter leaned and held forth a big fisted hand. He dropped the loads he'd removed from Abner's gun into the younger man's hand. He said nothing after doing this, he simply sat back and went on with his breakfast, and a little later, still sounding highly sceptical, he said, 'I'll tell you why I can't believe there's a town run by outlaws; I been one most of my life and I've never yet seen a bunch of them as could get along together. Maybe right after they've busted someone's steel safe or taken a bullion crate off a coach they'll get along because everyone's got plenty of money, but that don't last long, and I've seen 'em fight over just about nothing at all. In fact that's why I don't partner-up with fellers very much, nor look around for their company. The honest ones are dull as hell and the others are as like as not to shove a knife in your back when you're sleepin' just to steal another horse and saddle.'

Abner finished his stew and grinned. 'Then why are you partnering-up with me?' he asked. 'How do you know I won't shove a knife into your back tonight?'

Porter gazed from shrewd little blue eyes. 'You're sort of like me,' he said thoughtfully. 'You don't take it all that seriously. You take it as it comes and don't figure any of it's very gawddamned important—neither livin' nor dyin', nor all the things folks do in between. You aren't a killer, Abner, any more than I am.'

They left Abner's campside with the sun just rising and with a breath of cold fog lingering miasma-like in several of the nearby low canyons. Porter asked their direction and when Abner was vague the older man ran bent fingers through his bushy beard and said nothing as he studied the far-away eminences.

They had good travelling for the morning and in the afternoon their only inconvenience occurred when they rounded a bend upon a sidehill of stones and skimpy trees and came face-to-face with a bear as black as original sin, and when he scented them and reared up looked to be at least seven feet tall.

Abner was behind. Porter's big brown horse swapped ends so suddenly his rider did not have a chance to remain in the saddle. Even if Porter Sunday had been forewarned he could not have kept his balance. Abner, who had ridden his share of end-swapping and sunfishing horses was impressed right up until the terrified brown horse charged headlong at him and his horse on the narrow trail. Abner could not yield because there was an abrupt uphill-slope on his left and an even more abrupt downhill-slope on his right, so he dug his horse with spurs and catapulted him directly ahead into a bone-bruising collision. The bay horse was flung back on his haunches even though he was the larger of the two animals. Abner's split-second thinking had told him not to wait to be struck by that big brown horse coming at him like an overweight cannonball, but to minimise the jolt by closing as much distance as he could. It worked. The brown horse was stunned and hung there, head down, reins underfoot, while Abner swung his animal half across the trail, palmed his Colt and fired three times into the shale at the huge feet of the big black bear.

Porter Sunday was dazed in the centre of the trail. The gunshots seemed to worry him because he flopped over onto his side and pawed for his own weapon. Abner bawled at him. 'Lie still and don't shoot at him, damn it!'

The bear, with so much activity confronting him, and with particles of sharp stone stinging his lower legs, weaved back and forth, squinted and wrinkled his nose and finally roared in distress when those stinging stone particles continued to draw blood from his lower legs. Finally, he dropped to all fours, plunged over the edge of the drop-off and went roaring and whining on his way downward.

Abner swung off, caught the brown horse and walked over to see if Sunday had been injured by his tumble. He hadn't, but he had been stunned by the fall and only very gradually recovered. With Abner's help he got to his feet, felt his legs and back, looked over where the bear was careering downhill amid a minor landslide of his own making, and said, 'By gawd, I'm going to shave first chance I get! That son of a bitch looked like a feller I used to know who also had a full beard . . . How did you do it; did you wound him?'

'No; peppered him with sharp stones. Why would I want to kill him, he was just walking along too.'

Porter leaned to look again, and shook his head. 'Well; the blasted furry outfit had ought to stick to bear trails.'

Abner rolled a smoke and studied the horses. They did not seem much the worse for all the excitement. The saddle on Sunday's brown gelding was far off-centre but that wouldn't take more than a moment to correct. As he lit up and exhaled, casting a final look down the slope, he said, 'Well, Mister Sunday, I'll guess that we pretty well announced our coming. Those gunshots would be audible one hell of a long ways.'

Porter was not interested. He said, 'That damned critter reared up and was fixing to launch himself at me. I never saw a bear go into action so quick. Usually, they faunch and bellow and try to bluff you out, but this one, by gawd, he reared up right now and was—'

'Let's get on with it,' said Abner. 'You better reset that saddle.'

They were a mile onward before Port seemed fully to recover, to look as confident and calm as he usually seemed, and by then he was willing to give some thought to that remark Abner had made back there, and which he had not answered.

He squinted into the off-centre sun, satisfied himself about the time of day in this manner, then tore off a cud from his plug of chewing tobacco, and said, 'If this town's back against them far bluffs, no handgun in the world would ever make a noise to carry that far . . . Is that where this Outlaw Town is supposed to be?'

Abner waved. 'Somewhere back there, yes. If not east, then to the west.'

'Say; I'd hate like hell to have you direct me to the only water-hole on a desert.'

'All I know is what I've picked up over the years,' responded Abner with spirit. 'I've never seen the darned place either.'

'Naw, nor will you see it,' stated the big, bearded man, and lifted his hat to mop off perspiration and to then drop the hat back atop his mass of hair. 'It's a good thing I'm footloose. I'd sort of figured to cross those rims anyway, and see what's on the other side.'

They spent most of the afternoon following hog-back ridges which were not very heavily timbered, and the reason they chose to do that was because the terrain was becoming increasingly steep, forested and rocky. It was no longer pleasant to ride northward. There was an indication in the broken skyline up yonder that the territory some miles onward would be more open again, but for the balance of this afternoon they crossed from ridge to ridge, skirting the canyons where they could in order to save their saddlestock. It was an unfriendly country for the balance of the afternoon and even when they began an early search for a place to camp, they only barely found a place adequate for their needs, with good grass as well as water for the homes, and with deadfall dry firewood for themselves.

It had to be in a low place to satisfy Abner. When they finally found the site Porter piled off wagging his head in monumental disgust. 'Who'n'ell's going to see firelight in this gawd-forsaken place, Abner? I'll tell you I been watchin' the signs all afternoon and not once did I even see tracks of even a wild horse, let alone of a shod horse with a man on his back.'

This evening they ate out of Abner's saddlebags and Porter's disgust increased. 'Oily sardines? Abner, I quit eating them things when I was half your age and knew how to eat better'n some lousy grubline-riding cowboy.'

Abner was blunt. 'You complain too darned much, Porter. If you're not doing something dumb like riding up onto a black bear, you're bellyachin' about the food. In the morning, why don't you split off and take some other—'

'Hey, Abner, I was only funning with you,' boomed the burly man. 'Hell; I got to go the rest of the way just to see how you weasel out of it when there isn't any town run by fugitives back in here . . . You like to play cards? I got a pack in my saddlebags.'

They played the two games cowboys and rangemen of the south-west knew best, Twenty-one and Pedro. Abner lost steadily.

No doubt about it, he had just learned something else Porter Sunday was experienced at.

Porter walked out a hundred yards or so from camp while Abner went over to look at the horses. When Porter returned as Abner was kicking out of his boots, he called to the younger man: 'Catch!' and tossed a fist-sized stone which had been painted an emerald green colour.

Abner looked up instantly. 'Where did you find it?'

'On the far side of this here ridge. There's a pretty good trail down there.' Porter scratched his cheek and looked a little chagrined. 'A while back when I said there weren't any horse-signs in the country we've been riding through?'

Abner smiled. 'On that trail yonder, where you found this green stone?'

'Yeah. And fresh.'

Porter sank down near his saddle, leaned upon the saddle-seat and twisted to cast a slow glance northward, but there were heavy shadows over against the bulwark-bluffs, and there were also fresh shadows creeping inexorably down where the men had their camp. As he looked back Porter said, 'Maybe we'd better not have a fire for breakfast neither; it was lucky we ate your sardines and didn't need a supper fire . . .Well; I can't imagine why any honest folks would be up in here. They'll have been fugitives like us, Abner, but maybe they did hear those gunshots this afternoon, and if so, maybe they're wondering where we are right about now.' Porter pointed. 'I'm going out yonder to bed down. If you're smart you'll hide too.'

'How many by the tracks?' asked Abner.

'Two . . . Just darned luck I saw that trail and came across the green stone. Well; maybe there is an outlaw camp up in here after all, but it sure as hell is no town.'

Abner smiled and said nothing as he picked up his boots and went gingerly across through the gravel and coarse soil in a westerly direction.

He did not know how far he had ridden, but he guessed the distance covered had to be better than twenty miles. In flat or open country he would have been able to cover that much territory in one day, but from the time he had met Porter Sunday there had been no great amount of open or flat country.

His final look at the bluffs where he thought Outlaw Town had to be, had been made before the sun had departed and those barrancas had still looked to be at least ten miles distant and more likely fifteen to twenty miles onward.

Distances were almost impossible correctly to guess in this kind of country and he knew it, but he also had the stories he'd heard over the years to suggest to him that the mountains were no more than twenty-five miles from the foothills down on the Bellsville range, to the heavily hulking bluffs which stood massively below the final rims, and it was mostly upon those tales that he rolled a smoke in the late dusk, lit up and smoked as he made his estimates.

Tomorrow they would reach Outlaw Town. He was certain of it.

From out in the distant darkness a booming voice said, 'Abner; you been baptised?'

He sat holding his cigarette and staring in the direction that sepulchre-tone had come from.

'Partner, if you haven't been baptised,' said the booming tone again, sounding more haunting and dismal than ever in the darkness, 'you're not fit to meet your Maker. Are you sure you haven't been baptised?'

Abner pushed out the cigarette against the gravelly ground. He did not know whether to answer or not; in fact he did not know whether to laugh or not. Finally he called back, 'Are you a preacher, too?'

'A brother of the Gospel,' boomed the deep voice again. 'A soul-savin' son of a bitch; Abner, I can help you get re-born. I can bring down salvation upon all your wicked deeds. Son, I can lead you into the valley of righteousness and anoint your mangy hide until you're as pure as the new-fallen snow.'

Abner said, 'Shut up and go to sleep. You want to know something, Porter? I've never ridden with a lunatic before.'

'Lunatic indeed! Abner, I'm going to show you the light come morning. I'll point out the way of clean livin' and straight shootin'. I'll bring an affliction of devils upon you so's you'll understand what powers I got.'

'In the morning, then,' called Abner. 'You're as crazy as a woodtick, Porter. Shut up and go to sleep.'

The big man groaned so loudly Abner was certain anyone within a mile would have heard, but then anyone within a mile would have heard all that other ridiculous talk too, so maybe the groan didn't make much difference.

The stars were pinned correctly into place, the moon which had been arriving a little later each night, did not seem to want to appear at all this particular night, and Abner decided he'd done a foolish thing not to bring along at least a couple of blankets because at this present altitude, grass and pine needles were not enough.

He got as comfortable as he could, lay back with both arms under his head staring at the magnificent array of stars, and tried to figure out what had brought on that sudden eruption of religious bombast. In fact as he lay there he concentrated on trying to figure out Porter Sunday. He was still convinced that as an outlaw Porter was treacherous. He had never yet met an outlaw whose basic flaw was not grounded in treachery of some kind or another.

Porter was a difficult man to read, and an even more difficult man to make sense out of, from listening to him.

Well; shortly now they were going to find what Abner had come up here looking for and then Porter would have his chance to be whatever he really was.

So would Abner, and he was feeling a little less certain about it all, as time passed.

CHAPTER EIGHT

ACROSS A BRIDGE

Porter Sunday was always the same, and that was unusual in outlaws. When he came back to their camp in the morning vigorously scratching, he grinned at Abner and said, 'Son; you never moved and that was wrong. You see, I did all that loud talkin' last night to let them know where I was so they could come skulkin' in upon me—only I was fifty feet away wrapped in a blanket like a damned In'ian, with a cocked Colt in my lap waiting for them.'

So *that* was what it had all been about. Abner snorted. 'So you sat up all night for nothing,' he said. 'I had no idea; I thought maybe you were serious about that religious talk.'

Porter sighed, shoved both hands into his shellbelt and gazed a little sceptically at the younger man, then he jerked his head and led the way across to the slightly downhill side of their gravelly ridge.

A hatless man was sitting hunched over there, tied with his arms under his hoisted knees. Abner had never before seen anyone tied like that, but he was more surprised to see the man.

There was a little blood on the side of the

stranger's head, matting his dark hair, and his black eyes were as venomous as the eyes of a rabid wolf.

Porter said, 'He won't tell me where the other one is.'

The prisoner glared at Porter. 'I told you and told you—there ain't no other one. I'm alone. I been alone all the time. I made a camp a half mile onward from here and—'

'He's the lyingest bastard I ever saw,' observed massive Porter Sunday. 'Mister, I told you before, there was two sets of rode-horse tracks.'

'The hell there was!' snarled the prisoner.

Porter sighed. 'The hell there wasn't.' He turned to Abner. 'I didn't sit up all night for nothing, did I?'

Abner stepped over, sank to one knee and despite the black-eyed man's hair-curling epithets Abner emptied his pockets. There was nothing much of interest except a carefully folded coarse square of paper. Opened out and spread flat it showed a fair likeness of the black-eyed man, and was a fugitive dodger listing a reward of five hundred dollars for the black-eyed man's apprehension and delivery to any legally constituted lawman. He was wanted in Kansas and Missouri for murder and robbery, and he looked the part. His name was Robert Burns but he also used a half dozen other names. He was clearly a hardened professional, and when Abner stood up reading that dodger, Robert Burns said, 'Well; you two don't look lily-white neither.'

That earned a smile from Porter. 'We aren't,' he agreed. 'But we don't skulk in the night trying to knife folks in their bedrolls neither.'

'Oh, hell,' growled the captive. 'I wasn't going to kill you. Only maybe take your money.'

'And the horses,' said Porter, 'and the guns, and set us afoot up in here without any way to even shoot supper. Bob, you're a lucky man. Other fellers wouldn't have just knocked you over the head when you leaned over their bedroll, they'd have busted your lousy skull like a rotten melon.'

Abner pocketed the dodger and considered their prisoner. 'You've got a partner,' he said, willing to take Porter's word for it that there had been two ridden horses on that trail along the far side of the ridge. 'Where is he—Mister? I'm not very good-natured in the morning early like this, on an empty stomach.' Abner lifted out his sixgun and cocked it while it hung suspended at his side. He and the black-eyed renegade exchanged a long, steady look.

'He went on,' mumbled Burns, avoiding Porter's knowing look. 'I told him we could clean you fellers out easy and he said he didn't want to run the risk of maybe doin' it to someone from Outlaw Town because it might get us in bad up there. Maybe they wouldn't let us in or something like that.'

Porter looked at Abner. 'No doubt of it; you look meaner'n I do. I got to admit it; you're a treacherous and ornery-looking individual.'

Abner ignored this comment to say, 'Burns, where is Outlaw Town?'

The outlaw looked surprised. 'Where is it? You two are headin' in for the first time?'

Abner repeated it. 'Where is it?'

'Untie me, gents, and I'll lead you to it.' Burns began to look less sullen.

Abner turned. 'He's your prisoner, Porter.'

The bearded man stood massively thoughtful and impassive as he gazed steadily at the trussed outlaw. 'I don't like his face,' he said. 'I figure we'd better just leave him here tied like that, and maybe pick up his horse and outfit on the trail and take them with us. Someone up in Outlaw Town might want to buy a fresh horse and whatnots.'

Burns did not act as afraid as he probably should have acted. 'That'll be the sorriest day of your life,' he told them. 'Anyone does anything like that around Outlaw Town, and they'll fix his spokes for good. They got laws up there, whiskers. You ride in and try to peddle someone's outfit that you plain-as-day got on the way in, and—well, hell—I've seen 'em get hanged at Outlaw Town for less. Whiskers, I'm doing you a favour.'

Whether Porter Sunday was impressed or

not, Abner was. He had heard rumours of this kind of discipline before. On general principles he was inclined to believe it. It would be hard enough to run a settlement inhabited exclusively by outlaws, killers and thieves and maybe even worse, but trying to run such a place without rules would be impossible, and not only with rules, but with the will and the strength to enforce the rules.

He gestured. 'Cut him loose, Porter.'

Abner expected an argument. Porter did not even look upset as he stepped ahead and began to untie the captive. When he was finished he lifted Robert Burns with one hand and held him the way a mastiff would hold a rat. He even lightly shook him before releasing his grip.

They let their prisoner sit and wait until after they had eaten their meagre breakfast and had brought in their homes, then they herded him along down the slope on the west side of the ridge until he reached his own camp.

At least he hadn't lied about that; it was indeed about a half mile onward. Nor had he lied about his partner going on; Porter read the sign while leaning upon a big tree studying the close-by ground, and when Burns had brought in his hobbled sorrel horse Porter told Abner what he had read.

Burns did not appear to hold a grudge against Abner but he certainly held one against big Porter Sunday, and in a way that was amusing because wringing wet Bums did not weigh a hundred and sixty pounds nor reach any higher than to Porter's mighty shoulder. Of course, that was one of the reasons for six-shooters to be called 'equalisers'.

As they turned back down off the lower clearing and reached the trail Abner saw another of those green stones, and tossed the one Porter had given him down at the edge of the trail, too. Burns saw this and cast an enquiring look at Abner but said nothing.

It did not enter Abner's thoughts that he was finally on the road to complete vindication. He and Porter could discuss that another time. Right now what Abner was interested in was his reception.

He still had not discovered that he no longer was carrying his badge of office.

The morning was cold but when sunshine came beaming across the endless distance to explode against those perpendicular barrancas below the pink-tinted upthrusts on the skyline, warmth followed almost immediately in its wake, and that loosened the muscles of the trio of horsemen.

No one spoke. Burns rode ahead, no gun in his hip-holster and no carbine in the saddleboot. Behind him was Abner and bringing up the rear was thick and solemn-faced Porter Sunday.

Abner was a curious individual but seldom curious enough to make enquiries when he was riding towards a goal which he expected ultimately to locate. This may have bothered Burns a little because now and then he would twist to look back, then shrug, straighten up in the saddle and keep going.

Finally, near mid-morning when the countryside was flattening out, turning broad and grassy and park-like with scatterings of huge old sentinel pines and firs, Burns pointed to a green-painted stone larger than any of the others and said, 'That's a mile-post. Whenever you pass one of them big green ones it means you've passed another mile closer in.'

'How many more'll we pass?' Abner asked, and Burns smiled as he scanned the onward rolling big countryside.

'Sure, can't never be sure, Mister. By now they've seen us. Maybe they've spoken to my partner and maybe he didn't want to mention that maybe I'd figured to raid a camp this close to town. And then again, maybe they'll just turn the stones on general notions that they don't like the looks of you fellers . . . especially old bear's-behind back yonder.' Burns pointed. 'See that big rock up atop the mountains where there's a couple of fir trees one on each side of it? Well, Outlaw Town is directly below that. Fellers who got reason to come here often uses them trees and that big rock as their guides.'

They covered another hundred or so yards and Burns drew rein a few yards behind a green stone. He looked at it for a long while. Abner had misgivings; he guessed that Burns's prolonged interest was probably prompted by the fact that this particular green rock should have been placed differently; he thought they were being told to keep right on riding and not to attempt to make the turn-off leading to Outlaw Town. He had reason to be worried; if this actually happened, then he had come an awfully long way and had run several risks for nothing.

But that wasn't what was holding Burns's interest. He dismounted, stepped past the stone to a tree and reached up as high as his short stature would allow to fish inside an owl-hole and bring forth a wadded slip of paper. Under the eyes of Sunday and Abner Wright he smoothed out the paper, read what was written on it, then started to pocket it. Porter held out a huge palm. 'Here,' he said.

Burns sauntered back looking murderously at the big man. As he passed over the note he said, 'All it tells me is that Wynn, my partner, didn't head for town but went on ahead to the apple orchard. He's got a hell of a thirst for cider.'

When Sunday handed the note to Abner, their prisoner sneered then turned to go to his horse. As he mounted up and turned in the saddle he looked more confident than he had looked earlier. In fact, the closer they had got to Outlaw Town, the more cocky Burns seemed to have become. Now, looking past Abner, he said, 'Whiskers; you're goin' to get it.'

Then he led onward before Porter could demand to know what that meant. But Porter did not look particularly upset. The only time Abner had ever seen him upset was when his horse had piled him in front of the black bear. Almost anyone at all could have been excused for being upset under those circumstances.

The day was warm, finally, and it seemed to be hotter in the hidden wide meadow country of the upland-mountains, probably as a result of heat bouncing off those perpendicular barrancas up yonder.

There was a brawling, wide white-water creek which had to be crossed, and here they found their first sign of civilisation; someone had done a very creditable bit of stone-masonry on both sides of the creek, and had then planked over the bridge with fir baulks which looked to Abner to be at least six inches thick. It was one of the strongest small bridges Abner had ever seen, and it was not only serviceable, it was also artistic.

He was surprised, not at the artistry because he had seen some amazingly creditable handicrafts by outlaws, but because this bridge was up where he had never been fully convinced there were any signs of civilisation.

They clattered hollowly across the bridge. From this point on there were no more green stones but half a mile ahead where there was a durable post-and-rider fence protecting a pasture where horses grazed, two large green-painted cedar posts stood, one on each side of the trail. From that point onward the trail widened into a pair of rutted wide tracks where wagons as well as riders could pass along.

Three men with tethered horses drowsing beneath nearby trees were up there in the shade on the far side of the green posts. They seemed to be idly talking, but now and then they would turn to mark the advance of the three oncoming riders.

Porter made a guess, which was not bad for him, since he hadn't believed any such place as this existed. He said, 'Hey, Burns; are those the vigilantes?'

Burns turned a venomous smile upon Porter. 'You'll find out.'

Porter smiled and said, 'You little scrawny bastard,' and ignored the pale and deadly glare he got back from their prisoner. No doubt about it, Porter Sunday had made a dangerously deadly enemy out of Robert Burns.

From this point onward Abner's concern was with his own personal well-being. He concentrated upon those heavily armed loafing men up ahead in tree-shade. He had known in his heart from the moment he'd left Bellsville two days ago that someone up in here was bound to recognise the man who was the law at the nearest southward settlement to Outlaw Town.

What he did not want, was for it to be one of those three men up ahead who were now, finally, unwinding from their slouching stances and turning to take an interest in the approaching riders. Abner wanted at least one good look at the renegade settlement before he ran into trouble.

Maybe there was a kindly Fate watching over him because when he was close enough he could not find a single familiar thing about any of those three armed men, and from the way they stepped forth to block the road, half smiling and also studying faces, they evidently had never seen Abner before either.

CHAPTER NINE

SUNDAY'S SERMON

The pock-faced husky outlaw who seemed to be the spokesman of Outlaw Town's roadside vigilantes, looked at Burns, at Abner, then at Porter Sunday, and suddenly chuckled.

'Hell,' he said to his companions, 'I know that feller with all the face-feathers.'

The pock-marked outlaw strode past Burns and Abner ignoring them to halt looking up at Sunday. 'How many times have I heard you say you'd die in the Chiricahuas; that you'd never leave 'em?'

Porter started to speak, checked himself and scratched, then started again. 'Why you lousy shirker,' he said. 'Dan Mallory!' He leaned to offer a hand, but the pock-faced man laughed and stepped back. 'No, you don't; you don't bust my knuckles. What are you doin' up here, Port?'

Sunday seemed to consider his answer very carefully before jutting a big jaw in the direction of Robert Burns. 'Dan, that little rat-eyed runt up yonder with no guns in his holsters, he tried to bushwhack me and my partner here, and I foxed him in the night and busted him over the head. He's got a partner come up through here a little while ago.'

Dan Mallory ignored Burns as he said, 'Yeah; we know his partner. We know Bob Burns too.' Dan turned. 'How close was you to the settlement when you waylaid 'em?'

Burns looked scornful. 'Close? Hell's bells I know the rules, Dan. I didn't touch 'em; didn't even chouse off their livestock, which I sure as hell could have done. Ask them if you don't believe me.'

'Come on, Bob, how close was you?'

'Dan, I wasn't ambushin' them. I heard 'em talkin' in the dark and figured they might be

93

lawmen or maybe scouts for a posse, you see, so I tied my horse and went back for a look. That was all I did. Ask that feller with the whiskers. I was lookin' them over when he busted me over the head.'

Dan Mallory turned back and Porter, gazing past at Burns, lifted his lip in an expression of plain contempt and said, 'Forget it, Dan. The son of a bitch couldn't successfully ambush a dead man. I heard him comin' about the time he started slippin' through the trees to find my bedroll.' Porter put Bob Burns out of his mind and broadly smiled. 'Dan Mallory, this here is my partner, Abner. Ab, this is Dan Mallory, I knew him down along the border for quite a few years.'

Mallory had a grip of iron and a tentative smile. He was a hard, ruthless-looking man, but at least for the time being Abner did not view him as an enemy.

Mallory turned to his companions. They both waved him off and went slouchingly through the heat to the shady place where their animals were tethered, turned each horse, stepped up and threw the men behind them a departing wave as they jogged off.

Mallory explained. 'When word is flashed from the heliograph points riders are comin' someone has to go out and look them over. Them two was in the middle of a red-hot poker game at Neilly's cardroom and didn't want to come, but their names was on the bulletin board along with my name.' Mallory shrugged. 'It never amounts to a damn, but we still got to do it. That's part of the regulations, and up here, gents, you obey the regulations.'

Mallory did not say there was an alternative to obeying, he simply said the men obeyed, and that was significant enough.

He gestured for Burns to go on ahead. 'Next time, Bobby, you're goin' to get skinned up. I know you are lyin' about how you raided these fellows. You've been fairly warned.' Mallory turned his back and missed the venomous black look he got as Burns reined away.

Porter fished forth a sixgun from his belt and handed it down, then he reached aft of the cantle and untied the carbine bouncing along back there and also handed that to the pock-faced man. 'Burns's guns,' he said. 'I could have busted his head. He's a lousy bushwhacker.'

'Maybe you should have busted it,' put in Abner. 'Every time he looked at you today, Porter, he wanted to kill you.'

Dan Mallory brushed that aside. 'Not in here. That's another rule.' Mallory grinned. 'We got lots of 'em, but you pull a gun on someone up in here, gents, no matter what the cause, and they'll bury you over against them brown cliffs.' He let that soak in before turning. 'I'll get my horse. First off, because neither of you have been here before, you got to talk to Mister Neilly.'

95

Abner remembered the name. 'The feller who owns the card-room?'

Mallory's grey, hard eyes kindled with irony. 'The feller who owns the *town*, Abner.' He walked ahead, got his horse and as they rode along he pointed to the horse-pasture. 'Two bits a day for your animals.' When they passed the first of the hewn-log houses he pointed to one with the door wide open and said, 'Two bits a day for housing too.' At Abner's look of interest the pock-marked outlaw smiled. 'Things ain't real cheap up here, but Abner, you're safer here than you'd be in your home-town jailhouse. No law stays in here. Now and then one'll come in and dependin' on who he is and how he acts, maybe he'll stay a day or two, but that's about the limit of it.'

Abner felt very relieved. 'I heard you hang them or shoot them on sight.'

Mallory looked pained. 'Hell no. What would we want to go and do something like that for? Abner, we keep out of trouble up in here. That's the secret of our success. No one is allowed to make trouble within a hunnert miles of here. Not even horse-stealin'. And if a man gets caught breakin' that rule,' Mallory smiled and kept right on lethally smiling. Then he said, 'That's what I was remindin' Bob Burns of. He knows better. He knows exactly what the rules are. But some fellers are just naturally bastards. He'll get it one of these days.'

Beyond the green posts the wagon road meandered across a very pleasant flat-to-rolling countryside and always in sight, closer now than before, were those straight-standing huge barrancas which closed out the northward world. They were so high a man had to tilt his head to see the mighty stone up there with the trees on each side of it which had been a pilot-rock for outlaws seeking this renegade's Eden for many years.

There was more grassy meadowland up in here than Abner ever would have imagined. Perhaps in prehistoric times an immense waterfall had roared over those cliff-tops and the power of all that awesome wet tonnage had blasted away granite and shale, had pulverised sandstone, had deposited deep layers of silt, and had created the flat-to-rolling huge meadow which ran east and west with patches of trees, with creeks and entire sections of lush grass and browse.

Abner guessed there was enough room up in here for several big cow outfits. Dan Mallory saw his roaming interest and said, 'Big, eh? I remember first time I came in here; I couldn't believe it. Never saw anything like this country smack-dab against them cliffs in my life and I've ridden a lot of back-country.'

They rounded a bend where huge cottonwoods leaned and the village lay dead ahead. Mallory reined up, lowered his hands to the saddlehorn and gazed up there for a moment before saying, 'You made it fellers. Welcome to Outlaw Town.'

The town was composed of log structures on both sides of a wide dusty roadway, and there were willows and cottonwoods along the roadway providing shade, and there were fruit trees, apples and pears Abner guessed, throughout the back-lots where the residents of the log houses kept their animals. There was a general store and a saloon, housed separately but under the same shake roof. There was also a forge and gunsmith's shop along with a harness-maker's store.

It was more nearly a village than a town, but it was larger than a great many villages so maybe it was correct to call it Outlaw *Town*. There was a burnt-cedar tree trunk as big around as a man set deeply into the ground not far from where Abner sat his horse, with a steel-bound sign on it, and there for the first time Abner saw the name of this hidden place in print. Someone had painstakingly burnt the legend OUTLAW TOWN into the flat, steel-reinforced wooden slab. Below that, with some fading paint someone else had crudely lettered another legend : 'Population 0, Ask Anyone.'

Porter laughed at the sign and got an appreciative look from Mallory who could still smile even though he must have seen this scribbling dozens of times. He jerked his head and led the way down into Outlaw Town.

There were several men seated in solid

warm comfort out front of a little hut which was a cafe. They eyed the newcomers and gravely nodded. Abner and Porter Sunday just as gravely nodded back.

Across, in front of the harness works an unshaven, raw-boned man squawked loudly. 'Port Sunday, you bastard!'

Porter looked, then called back a name and an even worse insult. He and the man who had recognised him loudly laughed.

They went past the cafe and saloon and general store to a log building with an ace of spades painted across the front window. Here, Mallory swung toward a rack, stepped off and tied his horse, then waited until his companions had done the same. Behind them a waspish, thin man with flaxen hair popped out of the saloon, looked, stepped out for a longer and more intent look, then ducked back inside the saloon again, unnoticed by the men Dan Mallory led into the card-room.

The place had six or eight round tables and right now not a one was being used, but there was a strong scent of tobacco smoke to indicate that no later than last night there had been games in progress here.

Mallory led them on through to a thick door with massive bolts reinforcing the six-inch planking. He had to lean to open the panel, but it swung inward without a sound on carefully oiled big steel hinges.

In the yonder room behind that assault-proof door were two greying, grizzled, stony-faced men, one leaning casually upon the mantel of a stone fireplace, the other man in a chair with four wheels mounted where the chair-legs were supposed to be. The man in the wheeled-chair was puffy-looking, overweight and pale, but his very dark eyes were like daggers.

The other man also had very dark eyes, and although he was not as heavy as the man in the chair, there was a marked similarity in build as well as in facial construction. Abner guessed they were probably brothers and he was correct.

The man in the chair wore no visible weapons but the other one had an ivory-handled Colt showing, tied down. He looked as though he were very capable of using it, too.

Mallory gestured. 'The one with all the hair on his face is Porter Sunday. Arkie Hannibal was in front of the saddle shop and recognised him. I used to know him too, down through the border country and in the Chiricahua Mountains. I'll vouch, Russ. So'll Arkie although I haven't talked to him about it yet.'

The man in the wheeled-chair considered Porter without saying a word for a long while, then he smiled a little and said, 'Welcome, Mister Sunday. Dan'll show you where to pay, where to toss your bedroll and where to turn out your horse.'

That was the extent of Porter Sunday's

initiation, apparently, because the man in the chair turned his attention to Abner, and at about this time a man slipped in from the rear of the room, walked boldly to the wheeled-chair and bent his flaxen-headed upper body while he whispered to the man in the chair. Then he turned without even looking at the others in the room and soundlessly went back the way he had come.

There was something Abner could feel, could sense. It hadn't been there before the fair-haired man had come and gone, but now it clearly was in the room, in the atmosphere of the room.

The man in the chair said, 'My name is Russ Neilly. That there is Sam, my brother.' He looked squarely at Abner. 'We got strict rules here, gents. No use of guns, no matter what happens, and no excuses if you use a gun here. You pay for your keep and the keep of your critters and you help with the chores of runnin' the town. Dan can explain what'll be expected of you . . . And if a lawman comes here without telling me or my brother who he is, there's a hell of a good chance he'll get buried here. We got a fair-sized cemetery east of town in the rocks . . . Mister; you got anything to say?'

Abner felt their eyes come around slowly to him. Evidently Mallory had heard this speech before and had heard it used on incognito lawmen because his friendly look and easy stance changed slightly. So did the stance of the black-eyed man over at the fireplace, the brother of Russ Neilly.

Abner was not entirely surprised that they had guessed about him but he certainly was surprised that they had managed to do it this quickly. Hell, he hadn't even seen the inside of the saloon yet, or the general store.

Porter Sunday fished in a pocket, brought something out and pitched it over into the lap of the man in the wheeled-chair. Abner stared. It was his badge! He wanted to plunge a hand into the pocket where he'd been carrying the thing. He didn't do it because there was no point in doing it; that was his badge, so it wouldn't be in his pocket.

Russ Neilly looked up at massive Porter Sunday. 'You knew who he was and you brought him in here with you?'

Port combed his beard. 'Well, sir, not exactly like that. When he was sleepin' I looked him over and found that in his pants pocket. But you see, Mister Neilly, him and me sort of figure a lot of things the same way; and hell, I've known a lot of lawmen who were worth their salt. Then there was something happened; he kept a black bear bigger'n I am from jumpin' on me when I was stunned and on the ground. Mister Neilly, you can turn me back if you're a mind.' Porter broadly smiled. 'I kept sayin' there was no such place like this and he kept sayin' there was. You can turn me back because I never expected to find any

102

comfort up in here anyway, so I won't be missin' nothing. But you've had a hell of a lot worse fellers in your town than this one is, badge or no lousy badge.'

Sam Neilly over at the fireplace turned to face big Porter. He was also a large man, but not in Porter's category. Now, he eyed Port with frank interest and said, 'Are you that feller from the Chiricahuas they used to call Grizzly?'

Port shrugged. 'That's one of the nicer things they called me down there, friend. What about it?'

Sam looked at his brother. 'He routed a company of Mex *Rurales*; I never heard of a man doing that before. They tell lots of tales about him.'

Russ was unimpressed; at least he did not show that he was impressed although he said, 'Sam, it's not the big one, it's the other one, the badge-packin' one. I already decided the big one can stay.'

Porter spoke boldly. 'Mister Neilly; I'm a feller as believes in payin' his debts. I owe Abner. I know it'll be no loss to you, but if you turn him out, why then I go too. And Mister Neilly, if you sic someone on him for bein' a lawman, well, sir, I give you my word the good Lord is settin' up there right now fixin' to be stunned out from under His crown over what I'm going to tell you, because I never before in my life did much to help a lawman—but you make trouble for Abner and you got to make some for me too.'

Sam Neilly listened, and shook his head and went over to a stove where there stood an old graniteware coffee pot. He drew off a cup as black as midnight and took it over to his brother. As he handed it to Russ and their eyes met, Sam faintly showed humour.

Russ took the coffee, tasted it in the lengthy silence, then said, 'Mister Sunday, so help me you should have been a preacher. We been thinkin' about holdin' Sabbath services out front of the saloon. Would you like to study up and preach for us?'

He did not smile and it was otherwise impossible to tell from looking at his pale, greyish and slightly bloated face whether Russ Neilly was being sarcastic, facetious, or just plain serious.

Porter studied the puffy face, combed his whiskers solemnly, finally raised his eyes to the other Neilly, saw Sam slyly wink, then Porter said, 'Mister Neilly, you're head-nigger up here. You say old Porter's got to preach and he'll preach. You say for Port to keep an eye on this blasted lawman and I'll make it impossible for him to find a knot-hole to pee through without me being there. I'm a believer in order . . . not law'n'order, Mister Neilly, but sure as hell order. For as long as I'm here I'll mind the rules and be your man.'

Russ Neilly sipped more coffee, and finally

104

his eyes showed something besides a haunted, shadowy look of pain and discomfort. 'I was joshin' about the preaching,' he said. 'Port; you're the windiest bastard I've seen up here in three, four years . . . All right, the lawman's your responsibility. Whatever he does, you're accountable . . . Lawman? Who are you after up here?'

Abner wanted to hedge but the sudden and swift way they had identified him made him fearful of being clever with these men, so he said, 'Two men robbed the Bellsville bank a few days back. One of them is dead and the other one, I think, came up here.'

'You know his name?'

'Yes, sir. Curtis Holt.'

Russ looked at his brother and Sam slowly shook his head. Russ then said, 'He's not here. And if he was he wouldn't be here long; we don't allow anything like that to happen so close to our town. Sheriff, you'd ought to realise by now we don't permit our people to raid in Durham County . . . Do you have a description of Holt?'

'Yes, sir—sort of. He's left-handed, dark, and has a little crescent scar over his right temple.'

Russ acted as though he hadn't heard. 'Show them to a house, Dan, and get them settled in.' Russ turned his wheeled-chair and jerked his head at his brother. They both went out of the room.

Mallory's look at Abner was different now, as he guided them back to the roadway and their horses. He was curt when he said, 'Lead your horses; I'll show you where to put them. Walk out in plain sight—Sheriff!'

CHAPTER TEN

TROUBLE!

After they had turned their horses out and had carried their gear to the twenty-by-twenty log house Dan Mallory had taken them to, Abner piled his riding gear and looked over at Port.

'When did you steal that badge off me?' he demanded.

Porter dragged his bedroll to a wall-bunk and unrolled it with his back to Abner. 'When? That first time we shared breakfast. When I come down and found you, the morning after you found me atop the knoll.' He finished unfurling the blankets and sat down to test the rope springs. 'I owe you a bottle of whisky,' he said, looking across at Abner. 'I never believed this place existed. It just didn't make sense, a town run by outlaws. Only that feller in the wheeled-chair, *amigo*, is the big honcho. I figure his brother, the man with the ivory-gripped Colt, is the enforcer.' Port smiled a little. 'Abner, someone was going to turn up

106

that badge sooner or later. Otherwise, they knew who you was anyway. Did you see that tow-headed cowboy come in and whisper to Russ Neilly? Well, right afterwards they all commenced acting a little different towards us—mainly, towards you.'

Abner stepped to the open doorway and leaned, looking up into the tree-shaded but sun-bright northward roadway. There was no point in making something big out of Porter taking the badge from him; not now. In fact, it was probably needlessly chancy for him to have kept the badge with him, anyway.

He said, 'Thanks for the support.'

'Ah, hell,' grumbled Porter, arising and shifting his gun and shell-belt, re-arranging the way they fit. 'Warn't anything. And you did keep that darned bear off me.' He fished through his things and came up with two sticks of jerky. He took one to Abner in the doorway and quietly started chewing on the other one himself. 'Tell me something I been wondering about, Abner : Did you just come up here to satisfy yourself there was such a place, or did you figure to find that left-handed feller who robbed your bank up here—or do you have some other reason for being here, you haven't talked of yet?'

Abner turned, masticating on the tangy jerky. 'You're awfully nosey, Porter, for a feller who stuck his head in a noose for a man he don't even know.'

Porter smiled a little. 'Son, that's why I'm bein' nosy. If you're here to try and spirit some fugitive out, I deserve to be told because they're lookin' to me to be responsible for you . . . Well, Abner?'

'I was hoping Curtis Holt would be here, but I'd also heard that anyone living here dassn't commit a crime, like Russ said, so I wasn't real hopeful . . . I guess it was mostly curiosity. I've heard about Outlaw Town ever since I came to New Mexico Territory. I was sort of like you; I just didn't see how any such a place could really exist.'

Porter accepted that. His expression showed that he accepted it. Porter Sunday was one of those people whose personal guilelessness made them transparent. No one would ever complain that they did not know when Porter Sunday was angry, suspicious, sceptical, or none of those things. But he offered one mild admonition as he said, 'If you're settled let's hike to the saloon. Lord knows a drink would set well . . . Abner, don't run no whizzers up here. So far I've seen two fellers who'd hunt a man to the horizon if they figured he had it coming, and I'm sure there's a heap more like that.'

They went outside. Across the road in front of another square log house a man was slouching in cottonwood-shade. He was thin as a cadaver with sunken dark eyes which were close set, and a long, hollow-cheeked face. He did not look well. As Abner and Porter set out that thin man called softly to them. 'Which one of you fellers is the law?'

Abner gazed at the stranger without answering. Beside him, in a very low voice, Port said, 'Word sure gets around in this place.' He too ignored the thin man.

They were out front of the saloon when a grizzled, unshaven lumpy man in soiled trousers and shirt came forth. He had a freshly-lighted cigar cocked at a rakish angle from his square jaw. He looked at Abner longest, then nodded at Porter and walked on without a word.

No question about it, Abner's identification had indeed got around.

The saloon only had about a dozen patrons, but if it had been down at Bellsville it probably would not have had any patrons this time of day.

The bartender had a white canvas patch over one eye. He was a large man fitted out in a fine brocaded vest. His one pale eye was not especially hostile when he said, 'What'll it be gents?' and when they replied that they would settle for beer he nodded and walked away.

The other patrons were as quiet as stones. They were elaborately uninterested, too, and that was also a dead giveaway. When the barman returned he said, 'This is a good batch of beer, gents; I just skimmed off the foam and dead rats and bugs this very morning.' Then he smiled. He was clearly indicating that they, Port and Abner, were welcome at his bar. They laughed because that was required of them, and afterwards they leaned and sipped beer and studied the other patrons—and a very unique row of side-by-side boldly hand-lettered WANTED posters over the back-bar.

The fourth likeness from the left was of Sheriff Abner Wright. The statistics were close to being right; they had him three years older than he was, but in height and weight and colouring they had him listed correctly. He drank beer and studied that poster, then studied the others. Two of those posters were black-bordered which he assumed meant that the lawmen listed there were defunct. He was wrong. When the barman returned and saw Ab looking up there, he casually pointed. 'Them gents with the black around their flyers has already been tried here—they call it *in absentia*—and convicted. If they ever show up here, they're to be hanged.'

Abner exchanged a long look with the one-eyed man, then solemnly said, 'Sure glad that don't apply to the gent listed on that fourth dodger from the left.'

The barman did not even look up; he knew exactly whose likeness was up there. He turned slightly and winked at Port, then laughed. They all laughed.

Some of the patrons looked up enquiringly, but none of them offered to come down where

Port and Abner were leaning.

The coolness was there, there was no question about that, but there did not appear to be any open hostility, at least none that was going to break forth into cursing and name-calling. The outlaws in the saloon knew who Abner was, and since this was a town where the law was not permitted to interfere, and not even visit if the Neillys had anything to say about it, a lawman could not expect to be received any better than Abner was being received.

He derived a little satisfaction from having got a laugh from the one-eyed barman, who had also to be a fugitive. It was not, he told Port, a bad start, and the bearded, big man finished his beer without commenting, and called for two more beers.

Dan Mallory walked in, nodded but did not come down where the newcomers were standing. He, instead, went northward and took up a leaning position between a pair of other men. The three of them talked in a desultory manner, the way men would do who had something on their minds besides the subject of their discussion, and a few moments later when they had finished drinking, the other two patrons shoved away their glasses and departed without a look down the bar.

Abner's impression of Outlaw Town was that while everyone seemed relaxed and confident and comfortable, they were also very much attuned to something—the conditions of their residency, or something anyway—and when Mallory or some other lieutenant of the Neillys came to give an order, the outlaws were poised to obey it.

Over his second beer he marvelled that a crippled man and his obviously gun-handy brother could rule the lawless deadly inmates of their town as well as they did.

That cadaverous individual appeared in the doorway, saw Port and Abner, walked on in and signalled for a drink, then approached the lower bar. As he hooked a boot-heel over the brass rail he turned and said, 'Abner, you're the law.'

It had not required second-sight to come up with that comment nor even the name that accompanied it. Abner pointed to the fourth poster from the left and the thin man glanced up there and glanced back. 'Good likeness,' he remarked, and shoved forth a bony hand. 'I'm Arnold McVey.'

Abner shook and jerked his head. 'This is Porter Sunday.'

Port ignored the extended hand. 'Doctor McVey?'

The cadaverous individual smiled thinly at Port and inclined his head. 'And for that reason you don't care to shake my hand,' he said. Porter was frank. 'You're plumb right, Doctor, that's the reason.'

Abner was mystified over this exchange. He

racked his memory and came up with nothing connected to a name such as McVey. The doctor accepted an unordered tall glass of red wine from the one-eyed barman and considered its dark and robust colour as he said, 'Sheriff, you're going to have to look at me as long as you're in town. We live directly opposite from one another down the road. And as soon as you and Mister Sunday walk out of here he's going to tell you why he wouldn't shake my hand. Sheriff; I'm going to get in my licks first.' McVey downed half his water-tumbler of red wine before continuing to speak.

'I was an army surgeon at El Paso some years back, Sheriff . . . There was a bloody skirmish down along the line. They brought back the wounded from both sides, ours and the greasers. They did that because the Mexicans did not have either a medic or a field hospital . . . Sheriff; I had one orderly and one nurse. The nurse's name was Mike Flaherty and he was as drunk as a lord when they started bringing in the wounded. There were sixty injured men, twenty-four of them barely clinging to life. I sorted them out and took only our men into immediate surgery. Later . . .' McVey downed the balance of his wine and turned with wet, bright dark eyes to smile mirthlessly. 'I injected—well—I gave a lethal injection to every Mexican who was, in my opinion, not going to make it . . . Sheriff; they raised hell. The army preferred charges and so did the civilian authorities . . . Sheriff; they weren't going to make it. Not a single one of them. It was said I'd deliberately consigned them to death by taking in only our surgery cases . . . That was probably true, Sheriff. It most certainly was true in many cases . . . Sheriff; I was an American, in the American Army charged with solemnly saving American lives . . . Tell me; which would you have concentrated on, Americans or Mexicans?'

Abner never had to answer. A flaxen-haired, pale-eyed dangerous looking man poked his head through the doorway and called. 'Mac; Russ wants you right away.'

McVey turned on his heel and instantly departed. Abner was again impressed with how a Neilly could call, and men dropped everything to obey.

Port tapped Abner's shoulder. 'He forgot to tell you something. Maybe he's forgotten it happened but an awful lot of folks down along the border know it happened; one of those wounded men they brought back was his son, a cavalry sergeant.'

Abner looked at Port. 'His son died?'

Port nodded. 'He died, and right after that Doctor McVey walked out of the surgery-tent and went down through the rows of Mex wounded giving them those injections he told you about. The charge wasn't neglect, like he sort of hinted, like he sort of wanted you to

114

believe, the charge was wilful murder of twenty-one Mexicans!' Porter paused, then reached for his half-empty glass. 'I got no more use for greasers than anyone else, but— not like that; a man don't do a thing like that to men who are too sick to raise a hand.'

Dan Mallory sauntered down and looked past Abner as though only he and Porter were against the bar. 'I put your name at the bottom of the list for scoutin' duty,' he said. 'Probably won't come up until about day after tomorrow.'

Porter studied the pock-faced man a moment then jerked his head towards Abner. 'How about him?'

'He ain't going to be here day after tomorrow.'

Port said, 'How do you know I'll be here?'

Dan Mallory's hard eyes narrowed slightly. He clearly was a bad man to trade words with. 'That's up to you,' he answered. 'If you need protection for a while, like the rest of us, you'll still be here.' Mallory finally looked at Abner. 'I saw you'n McVey talking. Well; that's about right.' Mallory started to turn away.

Abner reached without effort and hauled Mallory back facing him with one hand. 'Explain,' he said softly.

Mallory faintly reddened. He was a quick-tempered man, and fearless. That much was clear in his expression, in his hard, uncompromising eyes. 'I meant you'n that

115

lousy bastard McVey are cut from the same cloth.'

Porter straightened very gradually. Up the bar a couple of men who had heard that also turned and took an interest. The barman's one good eye rolled around to Mallory. He did not appear to approve.

Abner was not angry when he said, 'There's a law against me drawing on you. Right?'

Mallory sneered. 'That's right, but don't let—'

He never finished it. Abner's right fist came out of nowhere in a blasting blur and made a sound like breaking timber when it ground against Dan Mallory's exposed jaw. Mallory did not even gasp. His eyes flew aimlessly upwards, his legs turned loose and he went down without a sound.

The one-eyed barman leaned. Porter, catching movement from the edge of his eye, turned slightly and while his left hand reached for his beer glass, his right hand was out of sight. He said, 'Hey, barman, don't do that.' He made it sound more like an appeal than an order, but with his right hand out of sight, the one-eyed man straightened up and brought forth both hands to allow them to lie in plain sight.

Two weathered, faded, hard-faced men up the bar turned to look, then walked down closer and looked again. One of them had a scarred chin and left cheek. He said, 'That warn't the smartest thing you ever done, Sheriff Wright.'

The other one did not speak, he finished his inspection and walked deliberately across the silent room and out into the roadway to carry the news of what had happened.

Mallory's mouth trickled a little blood but not very much. He probably had bitten his tongue or the inside of his mouth. But he felt no pain.

Porter leaned and looked from squinting eyes. He said, 'Abner; either he's got a glass jaw or you got one hell of a punch. He's not going to come 'round for an hour.' Porter stepped over, and under the interested gaze of everyone in the room stood thickly astraddle Mallory while he removed the unconscious man's holstered Colt, shucked out every load, which he pocketed, then shoved the emptied gun back into its holster, and with a slightly apologetic smile to everyone, said, 'You boys know how mad a feller usually is when he wakes up from something like this. I just don't want Mallory to get himself killed tryin' to draw against folks who're out of his league.'

Sam Neilly walked briskly in, followed by that weathered outlaw who had hurried from the saloon moments earlier. Sam glanced at Abner from smouldering eyes, glanced at Port who was slouching upon the bar again, then stepped past without a word and flopped Dan Mallory over onto his back and leaned for a close inspection. He eventually knelt to gently wag Mallory's head back and forth and to otherwise make a cursory examination. When he seemed satisfied, he arose and sighed and scowled at Abner, then jerked his head for Ab to follow and without speaking, led the way out into the roadway sunshine. He hadn't opened his mouth since entering the saloon, and now he evidently meant to leave Mallory to the care of anyone inside the saloon who felt sufficiently concerned to help.

That happened to be Port. He got a half-tumbler of raw whisky and with everyone crowding to watch, cradled Mallory's head on his knee and poured in the whisky.

CHAPTER ELEVEN

ORDERS!

When Abner had first met Sam and Russ Neilly he had made his appraisals. Russ, he had thought, had reasons to be curt and perhaps warped in his judgements, and Sam, too, probably had reasons for looking as uncompromising and dangerous as he had looked.

Now, in the sunshine and shade out front of the saloon with Sam, it occurred to Abner that he was in one of those situations where he would listen and obey, and neither be asked an opinion nor expected to give one.

He was correct. Sam looked him directly in the face and said, 'Saddle up first thing in the morning and clear out.'

Abner paused over assenting. They looked at one another without particular animosity. Sam Neilly had passed judgement and had handed down the verdict. Abner finally said, 'All right. I didn't figure to break any rules. Mallory didn't give me much chance not to. Maybe on purpose to get shed of me, maybe just because he wanted to bait a lawman.'

'None of that matters,' said Sam roughly.

Abner half smiled. 'It all matters. But I'm not trying to beg off. You're the law here and I'll do as you say, I'll head back down the trail in the morning.'

Sam seemed to turn slightly pensive. 'My brother is still curious about you.'

'Nothing to be curious about,' stated Abner. 'I told you why I rode up here.'

'Knowing damned well you might get killed,' said Sam, sceptically.

'Not knowing any such a thing,' stated Abner. 'Personally, I figured you'd know better than to kill a lawman.'

Sam Neilly looked steadily at Abner when he said, 'You're more of a gambler than I am, Sheriff. In a town like this it could happen to you—to any lawman. My brother and I wouldn't allow it but sometimes things

119

happen here we don't get a chance to stop beforehand.' Sam fished out his tobacco sack and started rolling a smoke. 'That's another reason why we get uneasy about lawmen being up here. You're right about one thing. We don't want any killings; we aren't damned fools. Anyone with a lick of sense can figure out what'd happen to our set-up here if it got rumoured around that we killed lawmen and did other serious felonies up here.' Sam lit up and offered the makings. Abner refused so Sam pocketed them.

'It's not personal, Sheriff, about wantin' you out of here. We've heard about you lots of times. Bellsville's the closest town, to the south. As for Dan Mallory—he probably asked for that punch you gave him. We know Dan too, but you're still not welcome because you're the law.' Sam almost smiled. 'Hard feelings?' he asked, and when Abner grinned and shook his head, Sam said, 'All right. Then I'm going to tell you something.' He inhaled, exhaled, and did not blink his narrowed dark eyes. 'That left-handed bastard you're looking for came up here. We got ways, Sheriff, when we don't want someone here . . . We turned the stones and headed him on around and back through the mountains southward again. If you want him, ride south into the foothills, then go east beyond the stage-road. That's all I know. He's out there somewhere, still flounderin' around, so they told me and my brother, lookin' for this village . . . What really happened to his partner?'

'I shot him,' said Abner, and Sam Neilly nodded as though he had either already known this or as though he was not surprised at Abner's forthright answer.

Sam said, 'What about Porter Sunday, will he ride out with you?'

Abner could imagine no reason for Port to do that. 'He'll have to make his own decision, but if he comes out with me—he's wanted by the law.' Abner smiled, but his stare was uncompromising. 'I get paid to do my job, and I do it.'

Sam nodded. 'Good luck on the ride back,' he said, and turned on his heel.

Abner finally stepped into full tree-shade and rolled a smoke. He was aware that other eyes had been watching as he and Sam Neilly had been talking, and he'd never for a moment had any illusions about what those other men would have done to him if he had even so much as dropped his right hand to the butt of his sixgun. Now, he lit up, looked around, saw Porter come out of the saloon across the road and blew smoke. Porter started to stroll across the road. Behind him Dan Mallory also walked forth, but Dan did not act as though he knew Abner was over there. Dan turned northward and stamped in the direction of Neilly's cardroom.

Port stepped into tree-shade, moved past to

an old weathered bench bolted to the storefront behind Abner and as he eased down he said, 'You got marchin' orders?'

Abner nodded as he turned. 'First thing in the morning. How did Mallory act when he came out of it?'

Port looked annoyed at such a question. 'Well, now, how do you expect he acted, after someone had darn near cracked his jaw and knocked him stone cold in front of some other fellers? He was as mad you'd be or as I'd be.' Port tipped back his head and craned up in the direction of the cardroom. 'That lousy murderin' sawbones come out up there yet?'

Abner hadn't noticed; hadn't in fact, even remembered Doctor McVey. 'I didn't see him if he did,' he replied. 'Why?'

'Russ passed out and fell from his chair,' reported Porter. 'That blond-haired feller who wears his gun tied real low came in from the back-alley and told us at the bar. Russ Neilly, I'd guess is a right sick man. They got to talkin' a little at the bar, some of the fellers have seen him pass out and fall like that.' Porter leaned back, crossed an oaken leg over another oaken leg and looked into the roadway. 'You know how he got into that chair with the wheels onto it? He was robbin' a stage over in Deadwood and a gun-guard was inside the coach as well as being another one upon the high-seat, and he wasn't expecting it; the one inside cut him down with a shotgun. Miracle he didn't die, they say.' Porter raised shrewd eyes. 'Some gawddamn miracle! If I'd been in his boots I'd have rather died. He's got no feelin' from the belt down. Can't even haul himself upright and balance there. Dead from the middle down. Some lousy miracle, eh?'

Abner did not verbally agree, but he did mentally as he too glanced in the direction of the cardroom.

Dan Mallory walked out, and this time he glared across the road and southward. Abner watched Mallory without feeling much wariness. Regardless of what Dan Mallory might normally do to even the score between them, he would be governed by the rules of Outlaw Town. He would do nothing.

Porter said, 'Dan told me he'd never been hit that hard in his life.' Porter grinned in admiration. 'Sure glad you didn't swing on me.'

Abner turned away from watching Mallory. 'Tomorrow when I ride out,' he said, 'you'll stay on, eh?'

Porter nodded. He had clearly already thought this over. 'Yeah; but Sheriff, if a man can just overlook what you do for a livin', why you're not such a bad feller.' Porter laughed. 'That's what I told Dan. Leave you be, and after you'd gone him and me could settle in and maybe plot a little meanness.' Porter continued to watch Abner. 'Not in Durham County, though, so you won't have to bother us . . . Abner; too bad you're a lawman. If you'd just raid a coach a little, or chouse off a few head of someone's worthwhile saddlestock, you'd fit in and be a decent feller.'

Abner grinned. 'If I ever catch you in Durham County . . .

'You won't,' sighed the massive man, and sat a moment considering the scuffed toes of his worn boots. 'I got to catch my horse and take him to the forge and have that cast shoe replaced.'

'Damned cheap skate,' muttered Abner. 'That's a good animal. He's served you well, too. He deserves a complete set of new shoes all the way around.'

'I'm not made of money,' grumbled the bearded man.

'Then you're a lousy judge of stages and ranches,' replied Abner. 'We're only talking about a cartwheel.' He plunged a hand into a trouser pocket, but Porter saw the motion and scowled.

'I don't want your darned lawman-money; I wouldn't take money from a lawman if I was dying.'

'If you were dying you wouldn't need it,' retorted Abner indignantly. 'Get the horse shod all around.'

Porter agreed, finally. 'All around. Four new shoes. You sure make free with my cash,' he said.

Abner left Porter sitting there in pleasant

shade and walked out to the stone-fenced pasture where his horse was grazing with a number of other saddle-animals. The horse had completely filled out. Of course, he hadn't really been too tucked-up anyway. But Abner was pleased to see that there was no longer any sign of the rough country he had traversed, and walked among the other animals. There were at least a dozen brands he had never seen before. He felt confidently suspicious that at least half of those horses had been stolen. This was an area where almost anything a man encountered, including the people who inhabited it, were either accidentally or deliberately in violation of the law.

But it was a delightful setting, and it was peacefully quiet and serene. Ab turned back and strolled slowly back to the hutment he had shared with Port. When he came around the south wall to enter from the roadside opening Doctor McVey was sitting on a hand-made bench across the way drinking a water-glass of red wine. He called to Abner, who, with the balance of the day to do nothing in, strolled over.

'Wine?' asked McVey holding up his glass.

Abner shook his head. 'Never cared much for the stuff. Beer or whisky or nothing, Doctor.' He moved to a rickety chair and sat down. 'How long have you been up here?' he asked, and McVey cocked an eye at him.

'This is a bad place to ask personal

questions,' he told Abner, and got an indifferent shrug from the younger man. 'I've been up here four years,' he said. 'They got all the money I brought with me last year. This year I've been living on their bounty as Russ's physician.'

'How is he?' asked Abner.

Doctor McVey considered the sullen dark colour of his wine in the reflected sunshine as he answered. 'Well . . . not very good. At first, it's just their crippling debility, you see, but as time passes and they can't exercise, other difficulties develop, and such is the lousy engineering of the human body, Sheriff, that you can't simply have one physical ailment because there are invariably other parts of your anatomy dependent for their well-being on other parts. So—one thing leads to another. You understand?'

Abner understood. 'Yeah. But he's a young man.'

'That's all he's got in his favour from here on,' said McVey, and swallowed more red wine. 'That, and his very strong will to keep on living. But he's mortal, Sheriff. He's mortal—like all the rest of us.' Doctor McVey sipped more wine. 'You'll be leaving in the morning, eh?'

'Yes.'

'Well; I'm at least glad you arrived here and we met.' McVey smiled. 'Every man in this place has a bad flaw. Either in his character, his personality, or his brain. You're refreshing. But they wouldn't have allowed you to stay more than another day or two in any case. Your presence upsets all the others.'

Abner watched the last of the red wine disappear down McVey's gullet, got up to depart, and the medical practitioner reached inside his shirt and brought forth something wrapped in a piece of dark brown oilcloth. 'Sheriff,' he said, and held out the little packet. 'Something you can do for me if you will. When you get back to your town, post it. I'd give you money for stamps, except that I don't have any money left. Will you post it for me?'

Abner considered the packet. It was addressed to someone named Mary Jackson in New York. 'Yeah,' he said, 'I'll take care of it.'

McVey's sunken eyes glowed. 'I'm obliged . . . That is my daughter. She married a man named Jackson and moved to New York City. She probably has always thought I'm dead.'

Abner was surprised. 'You never wrote her before?'

'No; and have the government send in a U.S. Marshal for me?'

'If they're watching her mail they could still do that, Doctor.'

McVey crookedly grinned. 'Let them,' he said, and arose, bowed slightly and turned to enter his log house without another word.

Abner shoved the little packet inside his shirt-pocket and headed across the way. He made a guess about what was behind those last two words of Doctor McVey. If anyone would be an authority on the ill-health of a man even Port and Abner had guessed was in bad health, it would be the doctor himself. 'Let them' simply meant that Doctor McVey had kept that packet until he knew that if it fell into the wrong hands and government peace-officers came west in search of him, by the time they located Outlaw Town and rode up there, Doctor McVey would be over in the rocky cemetery west of town.

Later in the afternoon Porter drifted back to the log house. He had recently finished a big meal at the cafe and asked if Abner didn't want to fill up today so's he'd have some tallow under his ribs on the ride back.

Ab was not hungry. He said, 'Maybe later, along about supper-time.'

Port nodded. 'All right. I just figured maybe if we went up there now, there wouldn't be anyone at the cafe.'

Abner interpreted that to mean trouble. He raised an eyebrow. 'You don't have to wet-nurse me,' he said, and Porter answered instantly.

'Yes, I do. Sam Neilly told me to stick to you like a shinplaster until you ride out in the morning. He don't want anyone to get some notion they got to avenge Mallory, or just maybe to take a crack at you for the hell of it.'

Abner considered the massive, bearded

man. Already, Porter Sunday had been put into a slot by the Neillys; from now on for as long as the border outlaw remained at the Neillys' village, he would be at the beck and call of the men who owned the town.

CHAPTER TWELVE

'HOWDY!'

He and Port went to the cafe just ahead of sundown. There were several other diners there but no one more than glanced at Abner.

The food was mediocre but the coffee and the blueberry pie were excellent, and Ab bought two cigars, paid twice as dearly for them as he would have paid in Bellsville, and outside in the warm dusk he handed one cigar to Port and they both lighted off the same match, then strolled back to the hut.

There was no light across the way at the McVey cabin, but an hour later there was, and shortly after that someone over there played a sad melody on a stringed instrument of some kind. Ab said if that was McVey he was very gifted. Port's comment was a snort and a coarse curse.

Later, as Abner bedded down, he listened to the music with a more critical attention, and noticed that it gradually became less distinct and more blurred. He closed his eyes wondering if that red wine was adequate for blotting out the thing Doctor McVey drank it to blot out.

When the pre-dawn cold arrived Abner awoke and listened to the vast silence all around. He was reluctant to rise but now that he knew how much territory he had to cover, knew how to pace himself and when to start out for the best results, he forced himself to roll out, get dressed and head for the trough behind the cabin where he could wash.

The town was totally dark, but Abner had a hunch it was not as vulnerable as it looked. Not this town.

Later, he went to catch his drowsing horse and lead it up out front to be rigged out. He was as silent as he could be, and either he was silent enough or else Porter preferred not to have to go through a good-bye ceremony, because the bearded man did not move in his soogans across the cabin, not even when Abner walked the horse into the centre of the dark roadway, mounted him, and turned southward down through the cold darkness.

For an hour the riding was almost pleasant. It would in fact have been pleasant except for the coldness. After that he knew there would be a little dawn light to aid him in picking out the route he had used to reach Outlaw Town.

Somewhere off on his left, out through a thin stretch of tall trees, an owl hooted at him, and on southward a coyote yapped and sang, and got no response so he stopped his racket and hurried on, motivated by the same inherent urgency which made all coyotes hurry; they rarely ever walked, and they even more rarely remained long in one place.

Finally, there was a weak and unhealthy-looking grey brightness out along the far horizon, and by the time Abner was leaving the pleasant territory and beginning to climb into that rough, forbidding and darkly forested jumble of badlands, he could feel the strengthening new-day warmth beginning to make its way against the blue-black night cold.

A grey wolf with a widow's-peak of black hair evenly between his gold-flecked tawny eyes come to the edge of the trail and stood. He had every right to be afraid. Normally wolves fled from just the distant sight or the faint scent of men. This wolf might, another time, have acted that way but this morning he stood his ground and as Ab rode past, he and his horse exchanged a look with the wolf. His horse was decidedly uneasy.

Finally, a few yards onward. Abner turned in the saddle. The wolf was no longer in sight.

There was no genuine sunshine until an hour or more later. It had struck back along the cliff faces but where Abner was riding in the ageless forests it probably hadn't reached the ground in many centuries.

But he was satisfied for the warmth.

Sunshine-brilliance wasn't necessary, but sunshine-heat was.

He rode the first ten miles turning occasionally. Not that he expected to be bushwhacked—the same rule which prevented someone from backshooting him at Outlaw Town would protect him now, but as Sam Neilly had said, neither he nor his brother could prevent every violation of their rules.

But only one man back there, Dan Mallory, might have felt a genuine urge for revenge, and Abner knew Mallory's type well enough not to be very worried. Mallory might call him someday if they ever met again, but Mallory was not the back-shooting kind.

There still could have been another kind, though, and he rode along remembering what McVey had said about them all being flawed one way or another.

But there was no ambush. He got almost back to the place where he and Port had been waylaid by Burns and his partner without seeing anything even to make him speculate, and even then what he saw was a furtive rider westerly, staying to the half-mile-distant ridge and riding as though there were manhunters directly behind him. Whoever he was, he was not interested in Abner, who was parallel to him and a half mile or more eastward.

Clearly, Outlaw Town would have someone to replace Abner by evening. Abner made a smoke and rode through the delightfully fragrant pine-scented warmth, thinking of the reception that furtive man would receive. He remembered the faces he had seen and he intended to remember them; in his boxes back at Bellsville he was sure he would find posters of some of those men.

He killed the smoke atop his saddlehorn and grimaced. What could he do about it? If he found the poster for every man-jack he had seen in Outlaw Town including Russ and Sam Neilly, what could he do about it?

Nothing. Unless he wanted to be the instigator of a big, colourful manhunt with the army and a U.S. Marshal.

He compensated for the slight feeling of guilt he got from declining to consider a manhunt by telling himself that the inhabitants of Outlaw Town were governed by laws which prevented them from bothering his county, and that was the extent of his responsibility.

It was not, of course, the extent of his responsibility; it was never the extent of any professional lawman's responsibility, to be only concerned with outlaws in his own area. Abner spat, looked all around, and irritably changed the way he had been arguing with himself.

He was past the place where he had awakened to find Porter Sunday perched like a gigantic shaggy-faced vulture on Abner's saddle. He smiled at his recollection of that wakening moment when he had first seen Port sitting there, then he remembered that Port

133

had taken his badge, and he stopped smiling.

For some reason he was making far better time coming out of the mountains than he had made going into them. He had that ridge within sight on his left, the ridge where he had stalked upwards after finding the cast-horseshoe, and as the shadows began their late-day advance from the yonder west, he was beyond that rim which was about where he had thought he should change direction. He did, in fact, go another mile southward so as to avoid the up-ended territory around that ridge, then swung towards the eastern country. Over there, but beyond sight for the present, was the stageroad.

He was back in rugged territory again. It was difficult to look back, over where those barrancas arose, and imagine that an area such as the countryside around Outlaw Town, existed at all up in here.

But now he knew that it did exist.

A bull elk with a swollen neck walked majestically and fearless out to challenge Abner's use of the trail. It was not breeding season, but this buck evidently did not realise that; he was ready to fight.

Abner turned off to the right, passed down a narrow little brushy canyon, skirted far out and around and came up again a mile farther along. He had no intention of trying to straighten out the mixed-up psyche of some nine-hundred-pound bull-elk with horns big enough to pick a man and a horse off the ground.

Where he regained the same game trail the slopes all tended southward, so he rode around, into recesses, then back out and around again. In this fashion he finally achieved sufficient elevation to see the stageroad in the middle distance. It was too late in the day to reach it, and he had no reason for particularly caring to get over there anyway.

He grinned to himself. Porter might have felt an urge to get over there into the rocks at the side of the stageroad, but Porter was miles deep through the protective badlands.

He came to a creek and followed it hoping to find a clearing with grass for the horse. What he eventually found was a hidden log cabin about twenty feet square. He complimented himself both for the grassy glade where the cabin stood, and for the cabin, but when he swung down out front and stepped past the broken old slab door, he had to alter his plans for sleeping under a roof. The entire inside of the cabin was literally chock-full of twigs and ancient dust. Generation after generation of enormous woodrats had added a little more to their huge nest and now it actually filled the entire cabin.

But the horse would at least fare well. They made camp early, while there was still light to see by. The horse went out to roll. It had always been a source of great interest to Abner how a hobbled horse could teach himself to lie down, roll, and get back up again, with hobbles on.

The horse went forth to drink at the creek then to start feeding. Abner went after twigs to build a fire by. If he had to sleep outside tonight, without anything more protective than his sweaty saddleblanket, he intended to keep warm with a fire.

He, at least, was not very hungry, which was fortunate because he did not have much to eat; enough, though, to last until he returned to Bellsville, providing he was careful and also providing nothing delayed his return.

A large old battle-scarred badger came trundling through the late-day haze to snuffle at the cabin, at the salt-scented saddle, and no doubt he would have begun eating leather if Abner hadn't returned.

Even so the badger was disinclined to relinquish his rich discovery just because one of those two-legged creatures had arrived, and pound for pound there was no more fierce fighter alive than an aroused badger.

Abner pitched a couple of stones at him and the badger flattened and hissed but would not leave the saddle, and when Abner went over to lift away the saddle the badger rushed him, fangs bared. He finally got the saddle away, pitched it atop the lowest slope of the cabin roof, and ignored the badger who searched for a half-hour before finally abandoning his hunt in disgust. He went waddling off in the direction of the creek and Abner laughed at him.

Some passing coyotes ran into the glade, totally unsuspecting, instantly saw the horse, scented the man, and turned so fast they ran into one another. In their subsequent flight they were silent but fifteen minutes later they howled from the far side of the stageroad. It was a forlorn, distant sound in the gathering dusk.

Abner got his fire going, stacked enough wood—he hoped—to last through the night, and ate a meagre meal, made one final stroll out to make certain the horse was faring well, then went back to the front wall of the cabin, where the reflected heat bounced back, and got ready to bed down.

He would be warm enough, but in order to remain this way he would have to awaken every two or three hours through the night and pitch on more wood. It was no novelty; he had spent many a night like this.

The last thing he did was smoke a cigarette and the last thought he had was of the men and the village he had left behind, near the high barrancas.

The night semed short but that was probably because he was not totally rested when he awakened in the morning, because he'd had to awaken so often during the night to feed his fire. Still, he was rather well rested, and more importantly, his horse was rested.

He felt a scratchy jaw, guessed about how disreputable he looked in other ways as well, and went out to catch the horse and rig it out just as a golden sun arose majestically across a long, narrow treeless ridge to the east.

This morning it was not as cold as it had been previous mornings, and as Abner struck camp and reined off in the direction of the stageroad he cast a wary eye skyward. Sure enough, there were clouds drifting towards a rendezvous up there. It might not rain, but this time of year it was more likely that it would rain.

He studied the heavens with interest mainly because he did not have a slicker with him, and while a man could manage moderately well in New Mexico Territory in summertime without blankets at night and without heavy clothing during the day, there was no way to improvise adequate shelter from a rainfall in an area where standing under big trees was the only alternative to getting soaked.

He guessed, though, that the rain, if it actually arrived, would not appear until evening, and by then he hoped to be in a position to make a run for town if he had to. Bellsville was not too distant on the southward range.

The warmth persisted. When he topped out and saw the stageroad below and dead ahead, although it was early morning there were indications of heat down there.

Northward, but a long way up there, a thin spiralling upthrust of dust hung above a moving speck which would undoubtedly be the morning stage to Bellsville.

Abner looped his reins, rolled a smoke and sat comfortably in the top-out sunshine watching the stagecoach. It would be at least an hour before the vehicle got down where he was, and since he was not especially interested in it he would be over across the road by that time, looking for some sign of the outlaw named Holt he particularly wanted.

Southward there was nothing for a very long distance, until he detected sunlight on a few metal roofs where Bellsville would be. He smiled to himself over the men down there, John Lewis, the banker, Bowie the harness-maker, Hatcher, Farley, all of them, who by now would be muttering over the absence of their sheriff.

One advantage to being sedentary, he told his horse, was that you could walk out each morning into the pleasant sunshine in an orderly town, and curse the local lawman. Folks sometimes didn't have to have much of a reason.

He reined down off the ridge, picking his way through east-slope underbrush and later, a few forlorn trees. That stagecoach was still scuffing dust, which meant the driver was making his best time on the downhill grade.

When Abner reached the roadside he halted again, and sat a moment looking and listening. There was something close so he crossed over, passed from sight in through some huge grey rocks, whip-sawed his way around through high stumps where local woodcutters had gnawed away the trees nearest the road, and from there he began to cut back and forth, on a half-mile tangent each time, looking for shod-horse tracks. What he found was a fairly fresh camp and beyond that unshod horse-tracks. Not many travellers rode barefoot horses; not in a country where sandy soil and equally as abrasive shale could make a horse go tender in one day.

Out of curiosity, and out of the feeling that he had all the time in the world, he tracked those barefoot marks and passed through a second-growth stand of fragrant pines and came upon six Indians, three bucks and three squaws, making a camp along a creekbank.

He halted, then pulled back into deeper shade and shelter. The Indians had not seen him nor heard him, fortunately. He watched a long time. Clearly, these people had felt uncomfortable in their camp over near the coach-road. Probably with reason; they were supposed to be on Reservations. Neither the government nor the army allowed Indians to return to their old way of life in the mountains and out through the ancient hunting grounds.

These would be cut-backs.

The bucks were not especially young men, but they were tall, stalwart, muscular men. The women wore plaited jet-black hair encased in otter skins. They were clearly blanket-Indians. Abner saw carbines and sixguns, metal cooking pots and steel knives, but otherwise the break-outs were clearly following the old ways in attire, in the way they moved and even in the way they set up their hide-house-camp.

He would normally have skirted around without allowing them to know he'd seen them. And he would never mention having seen them. The reason he finally rode forth, palm forward, arm upraised, was because if anyone had seen a solitary, furtive white man in these mountains, it would be those people down next to the creek.

They saw him within seconds of the time he emerged from the thin fringe of trees. One of the women made a little trilling sound of warning. The three men stepped to their guns and hoisted the weapons to bent arms, and stood like carvings. They did not look solely at Abner Wright. They knew from bad and bitter experience that ordinarily the man who rode out with his arm raised, palm forward, was not alone, he was the scout, the forerunner of dozens of other armed men.

This time it was solely Abner. He rode on up, dropped his arm, shoved back his hat and said, 'Howdy, Folks.'

A broad-faced Indian who stood at least seven feet tall and looked even taller, answered in English, 'Howdy, Mister.'

They did not invite Abner to alight and he made no move to do it uninvited. Clearly, the Indians wanted this visit to be over with as quickly as possible.

CHAPTER THIRTEEN

CONVERGING ELEMENTS

The tall Indian had almost gentle, full features but Abner was not deluded. He had no idea what kind of tribesmen these were except that he was certain they were not Apaches nor even Pueblos nor Navajos. They were too large, were too different in attire, and when they said something, usually brusquely, back and forth in their own language, it was not a tongue he had ever heard before.

Finally, that very tall buck said, 'You are from the army.'

Abner could safely shake his head about that.

'Then you are from the Reservation police,' the big Indian said, and Abner took the initiative because sooner or later the big bronco was going to compel Abner to identify himself as a lawman.

He said, 'I'm not Indian-hunting and I'm not in any way connected with either your police nor the army. As far as I'm concerned, you can go where you want, I'll forget I ever saw you the minute I ride away from this creek. But I want your help in one matter. I'm looking for a dark-eyed man with a small scar over his right temple.' Abner indicated where that scar would be with his right hand.

'The man uses his left hand instead of his right hand, and he's about my size and build.'

One of the woman said something curt without looking up from her work at the creek-side. The big buck heard and nodded his head slightly without taking his eyes off Abner. 'This man is riding a brown horse?' asked the big Indian.

Abner had no recollection of having been told what kind of a horse Curtis Holt had been riding at the bank-robbery in town. 'I don't know,' he replied, 'but if you've seen a man who otherwise fits the description I've just given you, the horse won't be important. Have you seen him?'

The big Indian looked steadily at Abner without answering. One of the other bucks, standing back a yard or two, grunted something that could have been a warning. His companion, the third Indian, also grumbled a little.

One of the women at the creek-side looked up. She was very attractive, and looked younger than the other women, but that was difficult to be sure of because the women made a point of not allowing Abner to see much of their faces. This handsome woman had golden skin and doe-eyes as black as obsidian. She said in flawless English that they had seen a man riding a brown horse and acting furtive, but they had avoided him. She then said the reason she thought it might be the man Abner was seeking was because they had all seen the man's booted carbine on the *left side of his saddle*. They had in fact commented on that; the weapon was slung on the wrong side.

The very tall man turned, eyed the handsome woman, then faced Abner and curtly said, 'That is my daughter.' He made it sound as though he were annoyed at her forthrightness. Indian women very seldom took part in serious discussions among men. Abner admired the girl's beauty and thought she had probably learned more than just good English at some church-school somewhere; she had also learned to speak out.

He smiled down at her. 'Thank you,' he said. 'If your father is worried, he needn't be. As far as I'm concerned, I've never seen any of you.'

She did not return the smile and she did not thank Abner, she merely nodded and lowered her head.

Abner turned back to the big Indian.

'Where did you see this man who carried his carbine on the wrong side?'

The Indian pointed north-eastward in the direction of the higher hills. 'He was coming down from up there, somewhere. He was riding slowly and looking behind him often.'

Abner could have smiled over that. Holt had probably decided that somehow he had been led a long way from Outlaw Town; about the time the Indians saw him, he wasn't really acting furtive by looking back often, he was acting baffled and puzzled, and perhaps angry.

The big Indian turned, still pointing. 'He was bound into that country, which was where we thought we might go, until we saw that he was also going there.'

Abner gazed eastward and southward. If Curtis Holt had remained on that course, by now he would probably be mid-way on around through the curving mountains and foothills in the direction of town again. It was anyone's guess whether he would continue to risk riding in the direction from which he had come recently after robbing a bank, or not.

There was only one way to find out. Abner said, 'Where will I pick up his sign?'

One of the other men spoke gutturally. 'Go out,' he said, pointing due eastward. 'One mile, one mile and a half. Go back and forth. You will find it.'

The visit was finished. Abner glanced at the beautiful girl. She was looking away as were

145

the other two women. He looked at the pair of more distant bucks. They were eyeing him unwaveringly and coldly. He smiled at the tall man and said, 'I'm obliged. Good hunting. Don't go too far south, the army's down there along the Mexican border.'

The tall man said, 'You are a policeman,' and Abner nodded. 'I'm the sheriff of the county you're now in. My name is Abner Wright.' He grinned a little, closed his eyes, kept them closed and said, 'I can't see any Indians,' then he opened them.

The big buck had a ghost of a smile up around his eyes.

Abner rode around their camp, crossed the little creek and kept a course due eastward as they had told him to do. Once, from a low sidehill a mile onward he halted to look back. There was no sign of movement anywhere on his backtrail. He pushed onward and when he had covered what seemed to be an adequate amount of ground he began to sashay. First uphill to the left, or northward, then southward, or to his right. He rode at least five miles to accomplish all the policing he felt was necessary, and his reward finally showed up in some soft earth near a seepage-spring where a mounted man on a shod horse had paused to dismount and drink, and afterwards to tank up his animal.

It did not have to be Curtis Holt. In fact, Abner was half of the opinion that if Holt were

146

still in his county a week after raiding the Bellsville bank he could not be very smart. On the other hand, Holt could possibly have been concerned about his partner. It was not unheard of for outlaws to have strong senses of loyalty.

But it was also possible that the trail Abner now picked out very painstakingly did not belong to Curtis Holt at all. There were always riders throughout the mountains in spring and summer and autumn.

He had nothing else to do but follow those marks, however, so he followed them. If it turned out that he had tracked down some grubliner or some summer-loafing rangerider or some pot-hunter, then that would be the way things would have to turn out. All any man could do was what he considered the most probable course to follow to achieve some degree of success, and since life was an entire adventure based upon improbable odds, there were never any genuine guarantees. The sooner a man learned that and adjusted his life to it, the sooner he would be able to smile away disappointments and laugh at his own failures. Abner had a smoke near a fire-blackened ring of stones and let his horse graze with the reins dragging while he sifted in ash and walked around studying both shod horse imprints and boot-tracks. He laughed at himself; he was no tracker. Those Indians back yonder probably could have even told the hour of the day those tracks had been made, the size of the man and even the colour of the horse, but all Abner could determine was that whoever the man was he was following had made those marks, and when he caught his horse and rode onward, he was of the opinion that he was doing something special just by not losing the tracks.

There was a stillness to the air and the heat seemed to increase up to a point. It was not especially uncomfortable but there seemed to be an increasing degree of humidity, so in early afternoon Abner paused to make another long study of the heavens.

It was going to rain. He was ready to wager money on that by the time he'd finished his study of the misty overcast and the breathless hush that seemed to fill his entire world. Also, those lazily converging clouds he'd seen about sunup were by early afternoon beginning to pile up, to meld and form layer upon layer of weighty, dark cloud-stratas.

He shook his head. Normally, like all countrymen, he welcomed the promise of rain. Not this time; he was going to get soaked unless he turned off southward, forgot about Curtis Holt and made a run for Bellsville.

If he did that, of course, when he returned after the deluge there would no longer be any tracks to follow, and in fact, unless he increased the rate of travel he had been employing up until now, he would never find

Holt—or whoever was at the other end of those tracks—because the rainfall would wash away his trail.

He left the cold camp, riding more intently finally. The next time he halted to smoke and assess the area he was upon a long-spending mountainside where patches of trees offered occasional shelter but where otherwise unless he had taken evasive action by riding only where there was underbrush, he would have been visible for miles across the lower countryside.

Then he ultimately rounded that great shoulder of hillside and saw movement a mile or so ahead down where some aspens grew in a protective clump.

Instantly, he headed off the slope for the lower land, and decided to abandon the tracks and make a direct approach, and if he came out through the aspens to discover he was hastening to capture the wrong man he could always go back and take up the tracks again, but now it was beginning to look as though those converging layers of rainclouds were going to be responsible for an earlier-than-usual dusk, and that added to his anxieties.

Whatever he accomplished had to be achieved before the rain arrived.

He paused to select a safe and hidden route to the aspen patch, then trotted part of the way. He was able to cover the total distance without being in open country but in order to do this he had to come up and far around that patch of lacy little aspen trees, then make his final approach from the north-east, which made it seem as though he had originally come from that direction.

He left his horse back a half mile, hoping it would not scent-up the horse of the man down there in the aspens, and also hoping that strange horse would not, in reverse, pick up the scent of his animal.

He left his carbine back there too. If there was a confrontation, it was going to be at much closer range than carbine-distance.

Finally, he sank to one knee to look and listen. Like an Indian, his approach was not direct, but followed whatever course was available which provided him covering shelter, but when he was within a few hundred yards of the aspen patch he ran out of cover. The last twenty or thirty yards would have to be made through grassland without a single bush or tree to provide protection. But by this time he was close enough to see through the aspens, except on their most southerly part where they were thickest.

He located a grazing horse. It had been off-saddled but the sweat-marks were distinctly visible even over where Abner was crouching. Even the sweat-marks from the cheekpieces of the bridle were visible.

It was a brown horse, exactly the colour the Indians had noted, and while that made Abner more hopeful than ever, he was not entirely confident; seal-browns were not the most common coloured horses on earth, but they certainly were not the rarest either.

The horse was a blocky, muscular beast, not very old and not very snuffy; he finally picked up the scent of a man over across the grassland-clearing and raised a quizzical set of soft brown eyes. He stood perfectly still, little ears pointing, looking directly at the place where Abner was hiding, then dropped his head, switched his tail and resumed grazing. The location of a man he had never seen before did not trouble him in the least. Beyond that one mild indication of curiosity, the horse showed no interest at all, and for that Abner could have patted him.

A man passed through the shadows of tree-shade over yonder. It was tantalising to see his movements, his general shape and actions and still not be close enough positively to identify him. Abner palmed his sixgun and was debating whether or not to simply stand up and walk over there, at least walk as close as he was able to get before the man saw him and reacted one way or another way, when the man passed out from among the spindly little lacy-leaved aspens into sunlight and Abner saw him raise his hat to tip it over his eyes— with his *right hand.*

He waited, still holding his gun in hand, for the man to move closer, and eventually, in fact, the stranger did move, he went out where the horse was and quietly talked to his animal. It was easy to see why the horse was so placid and calm; the man who owned him was the same way, and he was clearly fond of his horse. When he turned fully to face the direction from which Abner was watching, he had a full black beard.

Abner stood up, said, 'Gawddammit!' and walked out where the other man could see him. By this time he had noticed the clinching determination : The stranger's holstered Colt was on his *right hip*, not the left hip.

Abner sang out in a voice of suppressed disgust. 'Good afternoon, friend.'

The bearded man turned without any show of trepidation, calmly eyed Abner, and called back. 'Good afternoon. Come on over and set a spell; I got some coffee on the fire.'

CHAPTER FOURTEEN

A PRISONER!

The stranger wore his hat low. He had dark eyes, was roughly the same build and height as Abner Wright, and when he smiled he showed even, strong white teeth through the dark beard. He eyed Abner with frank interest while he was approaching, and when they were close enough the stranger turned and led the way to his little fire where the coffee was simmering. The only thing he said, until they reached the fire, was : 'Wherever you left your outfit, Mister, you'd better have a slicker because it sure looks like rain.'

The stranger's own yellow slicker was draped over his saddle and bridle, back from the fire and in among the quaking aspens. He had also strung a lariat between two trees and had stretched a square of waterproof tarp over there, tying the corners out to form a tent roof. There were no sides, but in among the trees even if a wind accompanied the rain, someone beneath that canvas would be able to remain dry.

It was the comfortable camp of a man who probably lived most of his life like this; he had no luxuries but his essentials seemed like luxuries. Very few rangemen that Abner had known carried a piece of waterproofed canvas, they simply hoped it didn't rain on them and when it did they cursed and huddled under trees.

The stranger's dark gaze was genial when he said, 'You been stalkin' me long?'

It was a reasonable thing for a man to say who was suddenly confronted by another man, armed and on foot, but who had clearly hidden his horse-outfit before appearing. Abner answered with a little expression of embarrassment.

'Not long. Just since this morning.'

'Any particular reason?' asked the dark-eyed man.

Abner said, 'Curiosity,' and reached to accept the tin cup of hot coffee. 'Thanks. I been travelling pretty darned light.' He tasted the coffee and smiled. 'Pretty good, Mister.' Then he said, 'You got a particular destination or are you just riding?'

The bearded man seemed casual in his response. He filled another dented little tin cup as he said, 'Well; I expect all folks got a destination. Me, I'm sort of bound for the border country. Not for any special reason, except maybe to work the cow outfits down there—maybe take a job.' He looked up, holding his cup up. 'I don't mind workin' in warm weather, but snow and ice and freezing temperatures where I grew up in the Dakotas sort of ruint me for steady work; I don't even like to work all ridin' season in warm climates any more. Gettin' old and gettin' lazier.' He grinned through the dark beard. 'Lazier. I never set the world on fire working . . . You?'

Abner felt comfortable here. He rolled a smoke to go with his coffee and tossed the sack over without asking whether the bearded man smoked. A tough-hided left hand shot out like a striking snake and caught the tobacco sack. Abner smiled. 'I'm sort of like you. I worked the ranges and got my share of scars to prove it. It's not that I got lazy, I don't think,

154

it's just that I got to figuring that unless I wanted to end up getting turned off every ranch where I tried to get hired on, when I was fifty or so, I'd better find something else. Any horse's-butt can be a rangerider.' He exhaled smoke, sipped coffee and continued to smile as the stranger finished rolling his smoke and tossed the sack back. 'My name is Ab Wright,' he said.

The stranger lighted up, savoured smoke as he exhaled it, and matched Abner's smile. 'Bob Custer,' he said, then broadened his grin. 'No relation, Mister Wright; even before you ask, I'll tell you, I'm no relation to the general. He come from Michigan and my family been around Waco in Texas since anyone can recollect.'

The dusk was settling, that peculiar stillness which seemed to presage most downpours was over the mountains and the southward rangeland. It was warmer than it should have been for so late in the day, and although it actually was a little early to make a judgement based upon the mealy look of the obscure stars, Abner looked up and sighed, then arose saying he'd better go get his horse and outfit.

He halted a hundred yards out, but the man at the little fire was still visible as a thick silhouette where he remained hunkering with his coffee and his smoke.

Abner got the horse and started back. A light, low wind came from the north-west. It passed along warmly and there was no follow-up to it. After it had passed, the land seemed warmer and more hushed than ever. It also smelled of brimstone, the way it sometimes smelled just before a downpour.

He was so certain that rain would shortly inundate the mountains and foothills he instinctively hunched his back and pulled down his hatbrim, and when he got back to the fire and the cheerful little camp and turned to off-saddle, he called casually to the hunched man still sitting thoughtfully drinking coffee, that he'd be willing to bet a new Stetson hat they'd be swimming in mud by morning.

Custer laughed and flung away sediment from his tin cup. 'Nope, Mister Wright, we'll be bone-dry. I figured this camp would have to shed water that's why I picked a higher place than the surroundin' territory, and in among these aspens where I could stretch my canvas. No water's goin' to get us, unless there is one hell of a wind come with it, and that don't happen very often.'

He got down on his knees in front of the fire and poked at food he put in a black-iron skillet not much larger than a big man's outstretched hand. 'You like refried hash?' he asked, and chuckled. 'You sure better like it.'

Abner strolled to the fire after turning his horse out, hobbled. He was hungry enough to gnaw the tail off a skunk if someone would hold its head, and said so.

Bob Custer nodded understandingly, then cocked a dark eye. 'How come you to be travellin' so light,' he asked. 'No slicker, no saddlebags full of grub, no bedroll—but two guns.' The black eyes were not the least bit suspicious, but they were noticeably sardonic, and before Abner could answer Custer also said, 'Mister Wright; it's none of my damned business. I know that, and I'm not asking because I'm nosey, I'm just sort of interested in someone who might be as interested in seein' fresh country as I am.'

Abner sat down, relaxed with his legs crossed, and let campfire heat soak through into his bones and muscles. He studied the man's beard-hidden face with its well-spaced dark eyes with the tugged-forward hatbrim hiding all the man's upper face and forehead even now, after dusk had arrived and there was no longer any reason for a man to want to protect his eyes from sun brilliance.

'Sometimes I travel fast,' he explained quietly, 'and sometimes I got to cover a lot of ground being light enough so's no one can overtake me . . . That answer you, Mister Custer?'

The bearded man stirred his refried hash with his left hand and balanced the fry-pan over the little flame with his right hand. He raised dark eyes and nodded. 'Yeah, that answers me, Mister Wright.' He kept genially regarding Abner for a moment before also saying, 'You'd maybe be surprised at how many fellers like that I come across ridin' in the back-country . . . What did you say your front name was : Allen?'

'Abner.'

'Yeah, Abner. Well, sir, Abner, you'd be surprised. Sometimes I get scouted-up like you done, and they come in to eat then slip away again, and sometimes they scout-up my camp and never come in at all, and I'll find their tracks in the morning.' Custer gestured with his stirring hand and arm. 'Big country, by gawd. I been sashaying back and forth up in there for a hell of a time. More'n a week by gawd.' He fell to stirring again. 'You know this country very well?'

Abner surmised the question which was going to come his way if he admitted to being familiar with the area. He said, 'Well; I've been around in it somewhat. Why?'

'Abner, you ever hear of a hidden settlement back in here somewhere called Outlaw Town?'

That was the question Abner had anticipated. 'Yeah, I've heard of it,' he replied, 'and in fact, I've known men who've spent some time in there.'

Custer pulled his iron fry-pan off the fire and looked steadily across at Abner. 'Where is it?' he asked bluntly, and continued to sit over there staring at Abner.

Abner vaguely gestured. 'North-west, I believe. I'm no authority, Mister Custer. I've heard stories about that place for a long while.'

'About green rocks?'

Abner smiled and gently inclined his head. 'You know enough,' he said, and the bearded man swore.

'Gawddamn it, I *don't* know enough. I thought I did. I been told when you find the green rocks and follow them they'll take you right into the place, and from there on out can't no law touch you.'

Abner held up a hand. 'Wait a minute. There is something else. They got a law up there which says anyone committing a felony within a hundred miles of Outlaw Town isn't welcome there. I also understand that if a man who is staying back there commits a serious crime while he's livin' there—they shoot him.'

Custer shook his iron fry-pan then took it off the fire and turned to divide the contents. He kept the skillet for himself and shoved the tin plate across towards Abner as he said, 'I followed those damned rocks for three days,' he said, acting as though he had not heard what Abner had said. 'You know what I think? I think them bastards up there re-arrange their lousy green rocks so's a man'll ride right on around through their country and on out of it again, heading down through this part of the hills. Abner, I'm tellin' you I been a gawddamned week huntin' that place and I've seen enough of those green stones to build a fence out of.'

Abner accepted the tin plate and began eating. He was not normally fond of refried hash, but tonight it tasted exceptionally good. The fact that he had been a long time between meals may have had something to do with it. In fact, as he lost the edge of his hunger he began disliking refried hash again, so that had to be it : He was as hungry as a bitch-wolf in whelping time.

For a while Custer, too, was content to sit in silence and eat, but he did not act very hungry. He kept eyeing Abner from the corner of his eye, and eventually he said, 'I never heard that, about them fellers at Outlaw Town not allowin' someone in who did something illegal around their territory.'

Abner shrugged. 'Then you haven't heard as much about Outlaw Town as I have, but for a fact I've heard that story from several fellers. Two of them who told me used to live up there at the settlement.'

The dark eyes still lingered on Abner. Bob Custer said, 'You ever break the law hereabouts?'

Abner looked up, swallowed and smiled. 'Well; maybe bent it. Maybe put a big crimp in it.' He kept smiling. 'You?'

Custer put down the scraped-clean skillet and reached for his coffee cup. 'I pick up an extra slice of cash-money now and then,' he muttered guardedly, and when Abner laughed, he raised dark eyes instantly, then slowly settled back with the cup and also laughed. 'Yeah, I busted the damned law hereabouts. But how the hell would those fellers up at Outlaw Town know it was me did it?' Custer raised his left hand and combed that luxurious black beard. 'This here isn't my hair. It's stuck on. And didn't anyone down there where I raided that cowtown get a decent look at me or my partner. How would anyone up in Outlaw Town know anything about me?'

That was a question Abner could not answer, but he knew for a fact that someone up in Outlaw Town *had* known about this man who was now using his middle name as his last name. The Neillys had known. They had told Abner where he could probably find Curtis Holt, the bank-robber who had raided down at Bellsville : Curtis Custer Holt.

He gave an honest answer to the outlaw's question when he said, 'I got no idea how they'd know, up there, but if you got led all through the mountains and ended up down here before the green rocks petered out—they knew, fake whiskers or not.'

The bank-robber bluntly said, 'I don't believe it.'

Abner offered no argument. 'Here you are,' he said, smiling, 'in the opposite direction from Outlaw Town. My guess is that you were probably pretty close to the settlement maybe day before yesterday. And this evenin' where are you?'

Curtis Holt, alias Bob Custer, drained his cup of black java and flung coffee grounds into the fire where a hissing, steamy reaction occurred immediately, then he raised a hand to punch back his hat and in the orange, flickering flame-light Abner saw the little crescent scar which had undoubtedly been the reason the dark man had been wearing his hat pulled down so low even after nightfall had arrived.

Abner said, 'You're a good camp-cook, Mister Custer. You can even make good coffee and that's not a common virtue among fellers who live in the mountains.'

The outlaw's disgust of a moment earlier probably was somewhat ameliorated by this praise. He blew out a big breath and held out his left hand. 'Sure could use another of your smokes. I been out of tobacco for couple days now.'

Abner did exactly as he had done before, and he noticed how that perfectly co-ordinated left hand shot out to catch the tobacco-sack, this time as he had noticed it shoot out earlier. He kept smiling as the outlaw leaned to work up a smoke, his white forehead glowing palely in the firelight.

'I reckon,' said the bank-robber, 'they could do it all right. I mean, they could have spies around, maybe down there in Bellsville and out through the hills and on the cow ranges. You're probably right, Abner. If they got a settlement up there, and they haven't never been raided or shot up or burst out, they probably got a good spy system and knew who I was and what I did.' He tossed back the tobacco sack. 'Well; how the hell do I get up there, despite what happened?'

'You don't,' stated Abner, pocketing the tobacco.

The outlaw inhaled, exhaled, and swore. 'Hell. How long do they keep a man out, like this?'

Abner had no idea, but he knew how long he was going to try to keep Curtis Custer Holt out of Outlaw Town—and any other town. He said, 'I don't know that much about their rules, Curtis,' and without any haste at all drew and cocked his sixgun.

The outlaw sat across the little fire with his eyes perfectly round and his mouth hanging open.

Abner said, 'The law,' and Holt squinted sceptically. 'You are the law?' he asked.

'Sheriff Abner Wright of this here county, Curtis. Do you want to know what happened to your partner?'

Holt did not reply to the question, he kept staring, and eventually he said, 'You nailed him?'

Abner nodded his head. 'Shed the gun and pull up your pants over your boot-tops, then stand up and put both hands atop your head and turn your back to me.'

Holt raised his trouser legs to show there was no boot-knife nor a hide-out pistol, then he lowered the trouser legs slowly and started to straighten up.

Abner softly said, 'Curtis, you try it and you'll never see morning.'

Holt let his breath out noisily, then reached far across and with his left hand pulled out the right-side holstered Colt and let it fall. That trick of wearing his left-handed gun on the right side had been the last of his disguise.

He sat and gazed at Abner Wright. 'I thought sure as hell all the time you was some feller from Outlaw Town sent down here to look me over, to see if they'd let me in, back there.' He let those words dwindle, then also said, 'You weren't lyin' about my partner?'

Abner had told the truth. Now, he elaborated slightly. 'He was working at the general store and called himself Douglas Whittier. He had half the bank money in his saddlebags.'

'You killed him?'

'Yeah; in the horse shed out back of the rooming house. He tried for me first, in the dark . . . He *didn't* make it, and I *did* make it . . . Get up, Curtis, we've got a long ride ahead of us, and we're probably going to be soaked by the time we get down there.'

FIFTEEN

LAW AND ORDER!

That was a good guess about them being soaked before they reached town. In fact they had not covered more than two miles, and by Abner's rough estimate they had at least twelve miles to cover, before the first fat raindrops fell.

They were as large as silver dollars and struck hard, making an individually noticeable sound, at first, then they began falling with increasing force.

The bank-robber had both hands tied to the gullet of his saddle. Abner had to get down and go back to put the man's slicker on him, and by the time he got back to his own horse the saddle-seat was wet; rangemen could tolerate a lot of discomfort and usually they said little about being rained on, but a wet saddle-seat was something they particularly disliked. Curtis Holt laughed from beneath his dripping hatbrim but Abner did not look around as he remounted and led off again.

There was lightning, too, but for a while it was a very considerable distance off. Abner watched it, counted slowly between flashes of lightning and the belatedly accompanying rolls of thunder to determine how far he was from the eye of the storm. His prisoner did the same thing and called out.

'Twenty miles. We'd ought to make it.'

Abner had no comment. He knew how fast a storm of this magnitude would travel if there was a little wind behind it. So far, though, there did not seem to be any wind. Not out where he and his prisoner were plodding along, anyway.

Holt was dry. A rangerider's slicker hung over his body and his saddle. It looked like an awkward and ungainly bit of attire and if a man wore one of them on the ground it *was* ungainly, but atop a horse it kept the man as well as his saddle bone-dry in the most dismal of downpours. He would sing out tantalisingly every now and then to bait his captor, but Abner was riding hunched with his head down and appeared to be deaf.

But even this variety of inconvenience had a good side; it was not a cold rain. It was not hot, but neither was it cold. Abner, who got wet very gradually as they rode southward upon the stageroad, did not really suffer as much as he would have if the downpour had caught him abruptly or if it had been sleety rain.

He had Holt's saddlebags slung across his lap and they provided a meagre variety of protection at least for his upper legs and at least for a couple of hours before the deluge worked its way beneath the leather too. Even so there was a sense of satisfaction to riding like that. Those saddlebags were stuffed with greenbacks. The remainder of the funds stolen from the Bellsville bank.

The storm was moving closer. There was still no noticeable wind but it must have been out there somewhere to bring on the full force of the storm as it was doing.

Once, in a lull, when Holt grinned and wagged his head, Abner said, 'You can't get but just so darned soaked, and I've been that way for an hour now.'

'You'll learn to keep a slicker rolled behind your cantle summer and winter,' replied the outlaw.

Abner looked over. 'Maybe. But we all don't learn our lessons, do we?'

This reference to the outlaw's captivity did not escape Holt's understanding. He stopped teasing Abner for a while and rode along looking bleak.

They had town in sight. They had some kind of a gathering of late-night lights in sight, at any rate, and Abner was hoping very hard it was indeed Bellsville, when the lightning streaks came closer, making the night-darkness crackle. It was like watching the sudden disclosure of enormous white veins across the high, black firmament, and each time those crackling white networks of electricity appeared the air became increasingly charged with raw energy.

Abner was uneasy. He forgot about his

physical discomfort. Evidently the captive bank-robber was also uneasy because he kept looking to their left, to the west and sometimes to the north-west, which was the general direction from which those lightning flashes came.

The rainfall was now advancing visibly down-country in actual moving sheets of water. They could look up and see curtains of water moving one behind the other, southward.

It was no longer possible to converse, but Abner was not in the mood for talking and apparently neither was his prisoner.

The horses were bunched up under the lash of stinging rainfall, and water dripped from their bodies in constant rivulets.

Those lights Abner had seen ahead were suddenly no longer visible. He was confident it had been the lamps of town, and he was also equally as confident, now, that they were perhaps no more than a mile, perhaps no more than half a mile, from Bellsville, but the increasing intensity of the storm had completely blotted out those lights.

Thunder rolled and the ground underfoot responded with shockwaves. Reverberations ground-swelled to a quaking *crescendo* then diminished to the point of silence. The horses did not seem to be aware of this underfoot quaking. Perhaps their other miseries occupied their full attention, but it was hard to imagine most animals not being terrified when the ground under them began to buckle and pitch.

Lightning flashed over a clutch of huddled rooftops, limning the entire Bellsville community dead ahead. The town looked ghost-like; it seemed to be an eerie variety of superimposed opaqueness with shapes and forms. Then it disappeared back into the blinding downpour again and Abner raised a wet fist to rub his eyes. The flash had nearly blinded him.

The lead-shank loped round his saddlehorn drew briefly taut. He looked back. Curtis Holt was leaning sideways and shaking his head, which threw his horse off-stride and made the animal pull back slightly.

Abner shouted but rain caught his words and carried them instantly to the sodden earth. Moments later the wrist-bound outlaw regained his earlier composure and rode along hunched and gasping.

They finally saw a fence on either side of the roadway. To Abner it was a familiar and very welcome sight. They were entering town. But it was still not possible to make out lights until they had passed another dozen or so yards into town, then someone's hanging lamp out front was gently swaying beneath a wooden awning, like someone signalling to them. Abner thought that lantern had probably been hung out front of the saloon. If so, he was almost halfway along on his way to the livery barn.

The horses were no help; they had been walking head-hung with their eyes closed most of the time for the past couple of hours. If it had been left to them they probably would have continued walking right on down through town and out the lower end.

Lightning flashed so close every detail of the roadway was glaringly revealed for a fraction of a second, then came the deafening crash and roll of thunder, and this time, finally, their horses reacted, but the road was a river and they had no solid footing to help them, so it was possible for Abner to retain control.

He saw the white-washed front of the livery barn and turned into the yard out front. Down deep in the runway was another lighted lantern, and this one too was slightly swaying although there was still no wind.

Abner swung down, felt his booted feet sink into mud, and headed his horse towards the lighted runway, slapped its rump gently, and stood with the lead-shank to Holt's animal in his hand as he watched his animal go plodding the last few yards to safety. Then he turned, stepped close and yanked loose the rope which passed under the gullet of Holt's saddle. He retained his hold of it and puckered his eyes to look up.

'Climb off,' he shouted.

As close as he was to the other man, it was not possible to make out much more about

Curtis Holt than his general outline. But he saw the man's upper body lean as he kicked his right foot from the stirrup as he prepared to dismount.

The lightning came so brilliantly blinding and so cracklingly deafening that Abner had no chance to move. It was like being entirely encompassed in a burnt-smelling cold brilliance which went through everything he was wearing to tingle every nerve beneath his skin. Then the blow came.

He felt as though his prisoner had kicked him with every ounce of his strength in the centre of the chest. It was as though Curtis Holt had been awaiting this one last chance, and had seized it with wild desperation as Abner was standing next to the seal-brown horse.

The blow cut off Abner's breath and made his mind turn totally numb. He felt fully alight, as though he were some variety of electrical torch, then the incredible brilliance passed in a second and darkness rushed in.

He thought he was floating, though he had bumped something in mid-air, and did not even taste the mud nor feel it.

The rain was roaring louder than a huge waterfall. Even inside buildings it was almost impossible to hold conversations. Every sound was blotted out by the incredible and endless roaring sound. It had no echo because there was no room for one.

Thunder rattled every entire building in Bellsville and it stampeded cattle and horses out upon the distant ranges. Some local cattlemen would be weeks finding their animals.

Once, at the lower end of town a fire started in an abandoned tarpaper shack, but as white-hot and unearthly as the fire was, seconds later it was completely squelched.

Abner looked up, saw the reflection of light, saw movement and smelled the liniment before he had any idea where he was or what had happened. He probably would have been much longer guessing what had happened if the liveryman wasn't leaning down yelling in his ear something about being struck by a tremendously brilliant and veiny sheet of lightning.

Someone lifted his head and poured down some green whisky which was like swallowing fire. Abner raised a hand to push the bottle back and a grinning face looked into his clearing vision as Lester said, 'Hey, Sheriff; if you'd had a cake of soap in your pocket you wouldn't have to take another bath all year. You're wetter'n a darned duck!'

A woman shouldered Lester roughly aside and leaned, her vinegary, faded beauty showing through no-nonsense lines. It was Miss Abbie. Abner recognised her. His vision had almost entirely cleared by the time she put a dry hand upon his cheek and said, 'Abner, can you hear me?'

He tiredly smiled. 'Yes'm. Some rain, isn't it?'

The hand on his cheek felt faintly warm. She said, 'Abner, it's a pure miracle you're alive.'

He suddenly remembered something and arched his back as though to rise from the harness-room cot. Miss Abigail pushed him down with the help of Lester and his nighthawk, and a couple of other people Abner had not seen until now.

He could not effectively resist, he was weak and shaky and his mouth as well as his throat tasted of brimstone. As he sagged back he said, 'Miss Abbie—my prisoner!'

She nodded and patted his cheek gently again. 'Abner—it's a plain miracle. Can you hear me all right, can you understand me?'

He said, 'Yes'm.'

'Abner; that lightning strike which knocked you fifteen feet across the yard and up against the front of the barn—killed your prisoner and his horse.' She paused, then said, 'Instantly.'

He looked at her face for a long while. They offered him more of that green whisky. He raised an arm this time with sufficient strength to push it away. He turned his head and saw John Lewis standing there wearing a black raincoat that glistened. Lewis was clutching Curtis Holt's money-stuffed saddlebags. He looked very satisfied. For some reason that expression bothered Abner so he rolled up onto his side.

Miss Abbie straightened back. 'He'll be all right,' she said through what seemed to be a diminishing roar of overhead rainfall. 'Let's just leave him. Lester, don't turn down the lamp. Now let's all of us go out of here.'

Abner slept. He did not remember dropping off and he did not remember the rainfall for ten seconds after he subsequently awakened, either, because there was not a sound and the sun was high in the fresh-scrubbed morning sky. Only when he rolled over and got both feet under him and stood up, feet squishing in water-logged boots, did he begin to remember a host of things.

He went out front. Someone had written 'Don't Disturb' across the outer half of the harness-room door. He got all the way to the front roadway in the warm and delightful sunshine without being noticed. People up and down both sides of the soggy roadway were more concerned with the damage to windows, to roofs, even to the rutted roadway.

He got almost to the front of his jailhouse when someone sang out his name from across the roadway, northward. Clement Bowie the harness-maker was over there in front of the saloon. He came loping across the road and Abner waited for him, then opened the jailhouse door and let Clement walk in first.

The harness-maker said, 'That was the

174

damnedest thing I ever saw. That feller was dead as a stone, him and his horse both, without a sign on either one of 'em.'

Abner went to his desk and sank down. 'Where are they?'

'The feller is in the ice-house until you're through with him then we'll bury him, and Lester taken a big team and hauled away the dead horse . . . Abner; there ain't no reason at all why you're alive and he ain't. How that lightnin' knew to hit him and to spare you no one'll ever know.'

Abner felt his bearded face, looked at his filthy clothing and said, 'Go on back to your shop, Clement. Thanks for stopping in but right now I got to get cleaned up. I'll look you up later.'

After the harness-maker had departed Abner yawned, felt his back because it was sore, and started to leave the jailhouse on his way to the boarding-house. The banker was coming down towards him still wearing the black slicker and there was not a cloud in the sky, the sun was dazzlingly shining, and except for the sodden look of the roadway and all the stores it might have been possible to believe there hadn't been a record-making storm.

John Lewis smiled broadly and shoved out a pale hand. Abner ignored the hand. 'You got all your money back?' he asked, and when Lewis vigorously nodded. Abner said, 'I'll see you later,' and shouldered on past. Lewis caught up and said, 'I only wanted to tell you how grateful we are, Abner . . . And that I never for a moment believed there really was such a place as Outlaw Town. I didn't expect my threats to fetch in the army and all to make you ride out like that.'

Abner gazed at the older man. 'Mister Lewis,' he said. 'Oh, hell, forget it!' And he resumed his northward way up through the sunlight.

He could see those distant barrancas. They looked even further away now than they ever had before from town, and they also looked purely primitive.

Inside his shirt he could feel the lumpiness of that waterproofed packet McVey had given him up there, and he thought of Porter Sunday, Russ and Sam Neilly, and felt a kind of personal kinship with them. He even recalled Bob Burns and Dan Mallory without as much antipathy as he had in his heart right now for the orderly banker of Bellsville, John Lewis.

He went all the way up to his room at the boarding-house wagging his head. Catching outlaws and recovering stolen money led a man into some very unique places and compelled him to meet some bizarre individuals. The hardest part of it was to sort out which were deserving of judgement and which weren't. As he turned to enter the boarding-house he looked back and saw John

Lewis crossing through the muddy roadway towards his bank. Even from that distance it was easy to see Lewis's look of smug complacency. If John Lewis spent all the rest of his life trying, he would never have the smile of Porter Sunday!

We hope you have enjoyed this Large Print book. Other Chivers Press or Thorndike Press Large Print books are available at your library or directly from the publishers.

For more information about current and forthcoming titles, please call or write, without obligation, to:

Chivers Large Print
published by BBC Audiobooks Ltd
St James House, The Square
Lower Bristol Road
Bath BA2 3BH
UK
email: bbcaudiobooks@bbc.co.uk
www.bbcaudiobooks.co.uk

OR

Thorndike Press
295 Kennedy Memorial Drive
Waterville
Maine 04901
USA
www.gale.com/thorndike
www.gale.com/wheeler

All our Large Print titles are designed for easy reading, and all our books are made to last.

22710